Boys and Girls Like You and Me

Stories

Aryn Kyle

SCRIBNER

New York   London   Toronto   Sydney

SCRIBNER

A Division of Simon & Schuster, Inc.
1230 Avenue of the Americas
New York, NY 10020

First Scribner trade paperback edition April 2011

SCRIBNER and design are registered trademarks of The Gale Group, Inc. used under license by Simon & Schuster, Inc., the publisher of this work.

For information about special discounts for bulk purchases, please contact Simon & Schuster Special Sales at 1-866-506-1949 or business@simonandschuster.com.

The Simon & Schuster Speakers Bureau can bring authors to your live event. For more information or to book an event contact the Simon & Schuster Speakers Bureau at 1-866-248-3049 or visit our website at www.simonspeakers.com.

Designed by Carla Jayne Jones

Manufactured in the United States of America

10 9 8 7 6 5 4 3 2 1

Library of Congress Control Number: 2009037972

ISBN 978-1-4165-9480-2
ISBN 978-1-4165-9481-9 (pbk)
ISBN 978-1-4391-0968-7 (ebook)

Some of these stories have been published in slightly different form: "Brides" in *Best New American Voices* 2005, "Nine" in *The Atlantic*, "Company of Strangers" in *Alaska Quarterly Review*, "Sex Scenes from a Chain Bookstore" in *Conversely*, "Femme" in *The Georgia Review*, "Allegiance" in *Ploughshares*, "Economics" in *H.O.W. Journal*, "A Lot Like Fun" in *Western Humanities Review*, "Take Care" on FiveChapters.com.

Praise for
Boys and Girls Like You and Me

"In every situation she creates, Kyle provides an honest look at complex relationships through her witty, honest, bittersweet prose."

—*The Star-Ledger* (Newark)

"What Kyle does best—and, lucky for her readers, frequently—is parachute into ordinary . . . lives and use her extraordinary talent to render them unforgettable."

—*The Miami Herald*

"Stories about the tender, terrifying path from youth to adulthood."

—*People*

"The complex emotional lives of women and girls are explored in this riveting collection. [Kyle's] haunting characters, with their vulnerability and cruelty, live on in the imagination. A strange, darkly humorous trip into the female psyche."

—*Kirkus Reviews*

"[Kyle's] short story repertoire is intelligent indeed; each piece is compelling and compact, with prose that creates a whole world in only a handful of pages. . . . They're everyday stories, but Kyle's succinct prose elevates them to a strikingly otherworldly status."

—*The Minnesota Daily*

"Kyle has written an engaging collection of tales. Fans of Lorrie Moore or Alice Munro's short stories will find much to appreciate in these moments of female experience."

—*Library Journal*

"This sure-to-please collection by Kyle probes the frequently wrongheaded choices girls and young women make to feel happy and loved."

—*Publishers Weekly*

"*Boys and Girls Like You and Me* is a superb follow-up to *The God of Animals*. The stories hit their mark often with unnerving disquiet—it's also the reason why they work so well. Aryn Kyle's latest work confirms her place as a wholly original talent in contemporary American fiction."

—MostlyFiction.com

"Kyle is writing to work out these odd, surprising, and often universal narratives, and for that reason with *Boys and Girls Like You and Me*, she continues to be a writer who rewards a reader's attention."

—*New West*

"Diving into the lives of characters full of angst, hope, and fear, Kyle has put forth eleven stories that will transform and inspire."

—*New York Journal of Books*

"Kyle takes an unflinching yet compassionate view of life, and when she writes of 'the feeling or knowledge or faith that somehow, someday, everything was going to be all right,' we come away reassured, with a new trust in human resilience."

—*High Country News*

"Aryn Kyle shows that she has somehow maintained a direct pipeline to the often irretrievable emotional states of childhood and adolescence."

—*The Gazette* (Montreal)

"In this absolutely knockout collection, Kyle channels girls (and women) on the verge—of making big mistakes, tumbling into the wrong kind of love, and reevaluating everything they ever thought they knew about themselves and the world. Brilliantly funny and moving, Kyle shocks and surprises in a voice that's indelibly her own. Loved, loved, loved this book."

—Caroline Leavitt, author of *Girls in Trouble*

"By turns mordant and tender, often comic, always precise, these beautifully written stories go to the heart of the oddity of what we call ordinary life. Kyle succeeds in telling bitter truths about her characters—both the sinning and the sinned against—without succumbing to bitterness herself. Hope and affection for our sad, bruised world shine through."

—Sigrid Nunez, author of *The Last of Her Kind*

Also by Aryn Kyle

The God of Animals

for Kevin

Contents

Brides

The first man I slept with kept his eyes closed the whole time. We did it in the prop room of my high school theater on the leather sofa my parents had donated to help me get a part in *Seven Brides for Seven Brothers*. It would have been better if my mother could have sewn costumes or if my father could have built scenery. But since my mother didn't sew and since my father said that he would rather drive a nail through his tongue than spend his weekend building cardboard shrubbery, they gave the theater department two hundred dollars for programs and the sofa we'd kept in the garage since our dog chewed through the armrest. And voila. Townsperson Number Three. I had a line too: *Somebody get the pastor!*

On the first day of rehearsals, I stood to the side while the rest of the cast members wrapped their arms around each other's necks and kissed each other on the cheeks.

"We're all *so* close," one of the Brides told me. "We're like a great big *family*."

The Brides and Brothers were all juniors and seniors and the rest of the Townspersons were sophomores. Our drama teacher, Mr. McFarland, didn't usually cast freshmen. He believed in working your way up.

"You learn by watching," he said. "Nobody walks in here a star."

Dilly Morris was the exception to this rule. A junior, she had been cast as Milly—the main Bride. Besides myself, she was the only person who wasn't jumping up and down and shrieking about how happy she was to see everyone. Dilly had been the lead in every musical since she'd started high school and there were stories about tantrums, about Dilly breaking props when she was angry, screaming at stagehands, making sound managers cry, and storming out in the middle of rehearsals. Supposedly, she had thrown her shoe at the tuba player during *Hello, Dolly!* when he repeatedly messed up that big parade song. And halfway through rehearsals of *Oliver!* she'd had Bill Sykes replaced for making farting noises with his armpit during one of her solos.

After we introduced ourselves, Mr. McFarland had us sit on the stage in a circle. We were supposed to go around and explain our character's motivations to the rest of the cast. Everyone else had done this before. I could tell. They didn't just have lines. They had histories. Jack Owens, who was playing opposite Dilly, adjusted his baseball cap while he talked about the hardships of living off the land. Jenny Crews's character milked cows. Lisa Anderson carried water from a well. And Allison Mosely had survived an Indian attack.

When it was my turn, I stared down at my hands.

"Well, Grace?" Mr. McFarland asked. "What's your character like? What do you want?"

I squeezed my fingers around my thumbs. "I want for someone to get the pastor?"

The Brothers rolled their eyes and the Brides giggled into each other's hair. Dilly stretched her legs out in front of her and leaned back on her hands.

"But *why* do you want someone to get the pastor?" she asked.

I tried to remember what was happening in the scene. "Because I hear a baby crying?"

She smiled. "Yeah?" she said. "So?"

My fingertips went cold and I could feel my throat tightening. Dilly leaned toward me. "It's because you don't think they're married," she said. "You hear a baby and you don't think they're married yet. Get it?"

I hadn't thought of that, but it made sense. It was a pivotal moment, then. In my single line, I was speaking on behalf of an entire history. Those frontier people were probably really strict about premarital sex.

"Thanks," I said, and Dilly winked at me. It figured that she would know about babies and religion and not being married. The year before, her older sister had gotten pregnant and dropped out of school. I guess it was a pretty big deal, since they were Catholic and all.

After rehearsal, Dilly stood at the side of the stage, whispering to Mr. McFarland while the rest of us gathered up our scripts and backpacks. The Brides stood in a cluster, nudging one another and nodding in Dilly's direction. I stepped closer to them, hoping that they would let me into the circle, speak to me with the silent language of their eyes. Suddenly Dilly laughed out loud and covered her mouth with her hand. "That's *terrible!*" she cried, and Mr. McFarland tapped her forehead with his finger.

When she turned and saw us, the Brides scattered and

3

I looked at the floor so that it wouldn't seem like I'd been watching her.

"Hey," she called and trotted across the stage to me. "Hey, you." She snapped her fingers. "What's your name again?"

I looked behind me, but there was no one there. "Grace?"

"That's right. Grace. You're a freshman, right?" I nodded. "Well, you did real good today." Her eyes dropped down the length of my body and I covered my chest with my arms.

"Thanks," I said. "You too."

"I really like your skirt," she said, and I looked down. "It looks like something Milly might wear, don't you think?"

Something fluttered in the back of my throat and I let my arms fall back to my sides. "You can borrow it," I told her. "If you want."

"Could I?" She ran her hand down the fabric of my skirt, gathering it in her fingers. "The costume department is absolutely grotesque. It's an embarrassment."

"I have others," I told her. "Better ones. If you want to come over and look." I thought of my clothes twirling around Dilly Morris on opening night, the fabric of my shirt touching her collarbone, the curve of her throat. It was the kind of thing I would be able to tell my children one day.

Dilly drove me home, and when we stepped through the front door, she stood lock-kneed in the hallway. "Ho-ly shit," she said. "Is your dad, like, a movie star?"

"He's a doctor," I told her.

"I feel like I should take my shoes off."

I sat on my bed while Dilly stood in front of the closet. "Jesus, Gracie. Look at all this." I could feel my heartbeat in the roof of my mouth. No one ever called me Gracie.

"My mom really likes to shop," I told her.

"I guess so," she said. "You're lucky. *My* mom likes to

watch infomercials in bed." She pulled out garment after garment, holding them up to herself in my full-length mirror and swishing her hips back and forth.

"This is really nice of you," she said and met my eye in the mirror. "You know, most people in the department don't like me much."

I tried to picture her nailing the tuba player with her shoe. "They're probably just jealous," I told her, and she nodded.

"That's what Mr. McFarland says too."

Dilly took out every item of clothing that looked old-fashioned and piled them beside me on my bed. I was getting used to the little noises she made in the back of her throat every time she saw something she liked, the clicks she made with her tongue as she pulled clothes off hangers, the way she sucked the air in through her teeth when she held them up to herself. But then her arm went stiff in my closet and her mouth pulled open like there was no air left inside her body. "Are these suede?" she asked and pulled out the pants I'd gotten for Christmas.

"Yeah," I told her, and she held them away from herself like she was afraid to touch them. "But I don't think they're something that Milly would really wear. You know, since it's during pioneer times?"

But Dilly didn't answer. Slowly, she held up one pant leg and touched it to the side of her face while she closed her eyes and held her open hand against her heart.

"But you can borrow them for yourself if you want," I said, and she reached out and took my hand.

"Seriously? I mean, really, seriously?" Her palm was cool in mine and I could smell her hair, sweet like cocoa butter.

"Sure," I said, and she shrieked as she clutched them to her chest.

"You know what I think?" she asked as she slipped off her blue jeans and stepped into my suede pants. "I think you should be my understudy." She pressed one hand to her pelvis and the other to the small of her back as she twirled in front of the mirror.

I felt the air empty from my lungs and I saw into the future, the way that everything would be: I saw us sitting on the empty stage, eating red licorice and running lines. Front and center, arms linked in the cast picture. Dilly having dinner at my house, spending the night, going on vacation with my family. No one would know her the way I would.

"But doesn't Mr. McFarland decide that?" I asked, and Dilly circled with her hands above her head.

"Gracie," she said. "You haven't been around long enough to know this, but things almost always work out the way I want them to."

During rehearsals, if she wasn't onstage, Dilly sat beside Mr. McFarland in the audience with her feet propped up on the seat in front of her. While the rest of us worked through songs or scenes, they would tilt their heads toward each other and whisper through their fingers. The background noise of their voices filtered through rehearsals and their laughter erupted during scenes that weren't funny.

The day after she came to my house for costumes, Dilly watched with Mr. McFarland while the Townspersons worked through our big scene. I tried to be in the moment, to feel the weight of what I was saying, to really *inhabit* Townsperson Number Three.

"Somebody get the pastor!"

When the scene was over, Dilly dipped her head toward

Mr. McFarland and whispered to him through her hair. He cocked his jaw to the side and nodded. "Grace!" he called, and I stepped to the edge of the stage. "Nice job with that."

"Thanks," I said.

"How would you feel about working with Dilly as her understudy?" In the audience, the rest of the cast widened their eyes at one another. "What!?" they mouthed. The Brides slumped in their seats and Jack Owens covered his chest with his hands and fell to the floor like he was having a heart attack.

"Okay," I said. "That would be fun."

At the end of rehearsal, Dilly came up and squeezed my shoulder. "Ignore them," she said. "The boys are morons and the Brides are bitches. Oh, and also," she said, "I saw this blouse in a window downtown. Cream-colored lace." She feathered her fingers down her torso. "It would be *amazing* for my ballad in the second act. Think your mom would buy it for you?"

"Maybe," I said. "I'll ask."

"You're the best," she said and hugged my neck. "The absolute best. You're going to be a great understudy."

And that was that. I highlighted Dilly's lines in my script and took notes while she was onstage. She started coming home with me after rehearsal. She said it was too hard to memorize lines at her house with her sister's baby crying all the time. We would sit on my bed and talk about the play, about rehearsals, about who couldn't act and who couldn't sing and what Dilly should do with her hair for the different scenes. I was her protégée, her faithful confidante, ready to step in at a moment's notice.

I imagined Dilly on opening night, deathly ill with some-thing really serious like tuberculosis or brain fever. I would hold her hand and brush her hair off her forehead while she twisted and moaned. "Don't worry," I would say. *"I'll* go on." It wouldn't be long before I was sitting beside Mr. McFarland during rehearsals and telling him the way *I* thought things should be. It didn't seem too unreasonable. Dilly wouldn't be around forever. *Someone* had to take her place when she was gone.

In some ways, I was better than she was. I knew the words to all the songs, for one thing. In the scene where she was supposed to be singing a lullaby to her newborn baby, Mr. McFarland had to stop Dilly mid-song.

"This is just embarrassing," he told her. "You don't look anything like a new mother singing her baby to sleep. You look like you have a migraine."

"It's because I'm trying to remember the words," Dilly snapped. She walked to the front of the stage, dangling the baby doll by one leg. "This is a retarded song," she said. "Can't we just cut it?"

Mr. McFarland stood up in the audience and the Brothers made a big show of diving to the floor. "Look out!" they yelled and covered their heads with their hands. "Get out of the line of fire!"

"I'm not cutting a song just because you don't like it," he said. "Learn the words, Dilly."

"It's so sappy," she moaned. "Wah, wah, wah. It makes me gag." She held the doll out by its leg and shook it at him.

"By next time," he told her, "I want to see a loving mother up there, a mother who knows the words, a mother who doesn't waste my time by coming here unprepared."

Dilly flung the doll out at Mr. McFarland and it landed at his feet. Everything went still and the rest of us waited while they stood, staring at each other. Slowly, Mr. McFarland bent

8

down to pick up the doll, keeping his eyes locked on Dilly's. They watched each other like two angry cats as he moved forward to hand the doll up to her. "I mean it," he said when she reached down to take the baby back. "Learn the god-damned words."

But during the next rehearsal, Mr. McFarland stopped all the girls before we had gotten to the lullaby scene. The Brothers had gone to a costume fitting and the Brides were trying to work through the wedding scene without them. Mr. McFarland paced in front of the stage.

"What's the matter with you?" he asked. "You're bland. You're boring. You look like a bunch of kids up there!" He looked at the ceiling and shook his head. "How do you expect three hundred people to pay money to watch you if you can't even hold my interest for fifteen minutes?" He hit his hand against the edge of the stage. "You think you can just show up and dazzle them? It's a job," he said. "You have to work for it."

We moved into the first few rows of the auditorium while Mr. McFarland pushed my parents' sofa onto the center of the stage and sat down on one side of it. "Okay," he told us. "This is an exercise in charisma." Some of the girls groaned and I turned in my seat.

"What is this?" I asked, and Allison Mosely shook her head.

"The worst five minutes of your life."

"Five minutes," Mr. McFarland said, holding up one hand with his fingers extended. "Each of you gets no more than five. Don't speak to me. Don't touch me." His voice dropped and he smiled out at us like it was a dare. "Just make me notice you."

He didn't make it easy. He didn't give anybody a break. One by one, the girls crossed the stage to sit beside him.

They smiled, batted their eyes, and played with their hair while Mr. McFarland stared out into the audience with an empty face. The harder the girls tried, the worse it was. Allison Mosely kept clearing her throat. Lisa Anderson tripped and asked if she could start over. Jenny Crews tried to blow into his ear, but her aim was off and all she did was make a piece of his hair stick up.

When it was my turn, my body went stiff and I couldn't find the right way to sit. I was all edges, all knees and elbows and knuckles. I traced the chew marks on the armrest with my finger until I had to press my hands between my knees to keep them from shaking. I tried to smile, but my lips were heavy and numb and I could see the other girls watching with blank, bored faces. I turned to face Mr. McFarland's profile, to catch his eye with the power of my mind. *Look at me. Look at me. Look at me.* But he didn't. In the audience, Dilly dipped her chin to her chest and covered her face with her hand.

When Dilly walked up onstage, Jenny slumped down in the chair beside me and looked up at the lights. "Here we go," she said.

Dilly crossed the stage like she was in no hurry at all and sat down beside Mr. McFarland without looking at him. Slowly, she extended her legs in front of her, crossing them at the ankles as she reached her arms up behind her head. She laced her fingers and pushed up with her palms until her whole body had curved and lengthened. She held the stretch, arching her back and closing her eyes as she tipped her chin from side to side.

"Shit," Jenny whispered, and the rest of us stared up silently.

Dilly slid one foot to the side and leaned forward to adjust the strap of her shoe. Her fingers moved down the ball of her ankle and traced the leather across the top of her foot. When she bent back up, she brought her leg with her, pulling her knee to her chest and circling her arms around the ridge of her shin. As Mr. McFarland began to turn, Dilly cocked her head slightly and rested her temple against her knee.

Everything went still. The space between them filled with something sharp and tight, something that swelled and spread and pushed all the air from the auditorium. I felt the rest of us shrink under the weight of it until I could feel them on my skin, on my lips, inside my throat. Until I thought I might drown in the space between them. They only barely smiled before they each turned away.

As Dilly walked off, Jenny held one hand up at the stage. "How fair is that?" she asked, and I looked at her.

"What?"

She leaned forward and shielded her mouth with her hand. "As long as she's fucking him, I don't think the rest of us can really hope to compete."

"That isn't true," I said, and Jenny rolled her eyes.

"Oh, come on, Grace," she whispered. "It's been going on forever." I shook my head and she sighed. "Sorry," she said. "I forgot you're Dilly Junior."

After we were all back onstage, Dilly linked her arm through mine. "I have a headache, Gracie. Want to fill in for me?" Her eyes looked heavy, like she was half-asleep, and she rested her head on my shoulder. It was the perfect chance to make them all forget how I had messed up the exercise. I took Dilly's place for the lullaby scene and she walked down and sat beside Mr. McFarland in the audience.

I knew the words perfectly. I rocked the plastic baby doll and sang to it like it was the only thing I cared about on earth. Dilly had never once performed the song like she meant it.

As I sang, I thought about the two of them watching me. I was sure that out in the audience Mr. McFarland was leaning into Dilly and saying, "Look at Grace. I had no idea."

As the song finished, I leaned down and touched my lips to the doll's forehead. It was a good move. Genuine. Maybe Dilly would even borrow it when she performed. The music ended and I raised my head to look out into the audience. But the seats were empty. I hadn't lifted my eyes the whole time I was singing. I didn't know when they'd left.

Dilly came home with me after rehearsal so that I could help her memorize the words to the lullaby. "I can't have you fill in forever," she said.

"How often do we have to do that charisma thing?" I asked, and she smiled without looking at me.

"Why? Didn't you like it?"

"I wasn't very good at it," I told her, and she looked up from her script.

"You just think about it wrong," she said. "Like with Mr. McFarland. If you walk out there *afraid* of him, you're gonna suck. It's the same thing with an audience. You have to think about power. You have it. They don't. You have to make them want you." She touched my shoulder. "Make them love you. Make them go crazy stupid if they don't get enough of you."

"You were really good," I told her.

"It isn't as hard as everyone makes it out to be," she said. "The next time we do that exercise, don't go out there thinking that you need to make him notice you. Go out there thinking that he's gonna beg *you* to notice *him*." She shrugged. "Be captivating."

"I don't think I'm a very captivating person," I said, and she tilted her head.

"Then pretend you're someone who is."

Dilly stared at the ceiling and tried to recite the words to the song. "Shit," she said. "This is hopeless. And I can't mess up again. He'll kill me."

"You and Mr. McFarland are pretty good friends, aren't you?" I asked, and her jaw tightened.

"I know what people say," she said. "And it isn't true, just in case you were wondering."

"I wasn't," I said quickly. "I wasn't wondering."

"Not that I couldn't sleep with him if I wanted to," she said. "He's head over heels for me, in case you haven't noticed. It makes him a little nutty sometimes." She smoothed the pages of her script. "But I'm not sleeping with anyone. And do you know why?"

I bit my lip. "Because you're Catholic?" I asked. "Because of God?"

"God?" she said. "I don't give a shit about *God*. Look at what happened to my sister. Did you know that she used to be a straight-A student?" I shook my head. "She could have been a doctor, like your dad. But not anymore." She sighed. "I've got a real shot at something, Grace. I'm not going to screw it away like she did."

"Do you love him?" I asked, and something in her face hardened.

"Love has nothing to do with it." She looked down at her knees. "He knows what I am, what I could be. He understands."

Dilly never forgot the words to the lullaby again, but it wasn't because she'd memorized them. She tried a few times, but finally she got frustrated and wrote the words on a tiny piece of paper that she taped to the baby doll's face.

"Look at that," Mr. McFarland said while she was singing. "Do you see that? I want to believe the rest of you as much as I believe her."

But the performance dates were getting closer and Dilly didn't seem to care about Mr. McFarland's compliments anymore. It was everyone else she was worried about. Nobody ever did anything well enough. We were clumsy, or off-key, or stepped on her lines. "I hate you all!" she would scream during rehearsals. "Just do it fucking right!" I waited for Mr. McFarland to step in, for him to calm her down or shut her up. But unless she was fighting with him, he didn't seem to notice.

Dilly seemed to enjoy pointing out everything Mr. McFarland had done wrong. The sets were phony, or flimsy, or put together wrong. The props weren't in the right places at the right times. The orchestra was too big, the backstage crew was too small, and the leather sofa looked absolutely ridiculous onstage. It was supposed to be the turn of the century, after all. Would they really have an Ethan Allen sofa sitting around in their log cabin?

Mr. McFarland paced and swore and held his hands up in defeat. "I've done everything I can," he told her. "What else can I do for you?"

She narrowed her eyes at him. "Nothing," she said slowly. "There is nothing else you can do for me." She turned her back and Mr. McFarland hit the sofa with his fist as he walked offstage.

They didn't say another word to each other until the last week of rehearsals when Dilly was working through her fight scene with Jack. In the middle of it, she pushed his shoulders hard with her fists and stomped to the front of the stage. The pushing part wasn't in the script.

"What now?" Mr. McFarland asked. He was sitting in the seat behind me, eating potato chips from the vending machine.

"He's supposed to be about to hit me," Dilly said, and I could feel Mr. McFarland's foot kicking against the back of my chair. "He looks like he's getting ready to serve a volleyball!"

Jack stood behind her and raised his hands like he was going to strangle her. In the audience, the rest of the cast laughed, and Dilly whirled around to face him. "Sorry," he said. "I don't have a lot of experience hitting girls."

"Have you ever watched a movie?" she asked. "A TV show? Jesus, it's not that complicated."

"Enough!" Mr. McFarland called, and they both looked at him. "Dilly," he said. "Stage right. Jack, stage left." They looked out with puzzled faces, but they moved to their assigned sides of the stage.

"Dilly," he said. "Try to get to the other side of the stage. Jack, don't let her get there."

On the stage, Dilly and Jack stared at each other.

"How?" Jack asked, and Mr. McFarland held up his hands.

"However you can," he said. "I don't care how. Just don't let her get there."

Dilly's body went still and I could see the veins in her throat, the tremor in her breath. Her lip quivered slightly as she looked out at him. "What is this?" she asked, but Mr. McFarland didn't answer.

"Go!" he said.

Dilly took a few steps forward and Jack stood taller, broadening his shoulders and holding his arms out to the sides. They watched each other's movement, shifting their weight and flexing their fingers. Behind me, I could hear Mr. McFarland's breath, faster, heavier than it had been a moment before. Dilly glanced out into the audience and then turned and ran toward Jack.

"Stop her!" Mr. McFarland called, and Jack caught Dilly around the waist. They struggled for a second, a tangle of arms and legs, and Dilly broke free.

"Come on!" Mr. McFarland rose to his feet and grasped the back of my chair. Jack looked confused, but he dived and caught Dilly by one leg. She pitched forward, falling face-down on the stage. The sound of her bare arms hitting the floor cracked through the auditorium.

"That's it!" Mr. McFarland yelled. I could hear Dilly struggling, her voice wet and wordless, the sounds of her body trying to get free.

Jack pulled Dilly backward by the cuff of her blue jeans and she flipped onto her back and tried to kick at his hands with her free leg. But Jack crouched over her, pinning her shoulders to the stage.

Behind me, Mr. McFarland kneaded the back of my chair with his hands until it began to rock back and forth under the pressure.

Jack moved to straddle Dilly, but as he did, she lifted her knee up hard between his legs and his head wrenched back as he fell onto his side. In a flash, she was out from under him and across the stage. When she reached the opposite wall, she put her hands flat against it and leaned forward, her shoulders heaving. She stood like that for a moment and then turned toward us. Her lips were wet, her forearms pink and raw where she had hit the floor. On the other side of the stage, Jack stayed crouched on his hands and knees, his forehead touching the ground.

Slowly, the cast turned to look at Mr. McFarland, who

stood rigid behind me. "Let's get back to work," he said. I kept my eyes on Dilly, but I could feel the heat of his breath on the part of my hair, the ridges of his knuckles against my shoulder blades.

The day of our first performance, Mr. McFarland called the whole cast out of first period. We gathered on the stage with our books in our arms, looking back and forth between one another for an explanation. When Mr. McFarland came out of his office, his eyes were red around the rims. He told us to sit down, that he had something to tell us.

"Dilly isn't here yet," I said, and he covered his mouth with his hand.

"I have some bad news." His jaw was clenched and I could see his Adam's apple trembling.

"Oh God," Lisa Anderson said. "Dilly's dead."

"No," he said quietly and lifted his head to look at us. "Her sister's baby is."

Everything went still and cold and my head felt heavy, like it had filled with water. I felt bodies stiffen on either side of me and Allison Mosely began to cry into her wrist.

"What happened?" Jenny whispered.

Mr. McFarland pressed his fingers into the ridge of his forehead. "They don't know," he said. "They just woke up this morning and the baby was . . . they just woke up this morning and found her."

"Dilly's not performing then?" I asked, and Mr. McFarland straightened.

"She won't be in school. But she'll be here tonight." He nodded to himself. "Dilly's a professional," he said. "And she'll be here."

That night, she didn't speak to any of us. A couple of the girls tried to hug her, but she shook them away. She sat alone at the mirror, putting on her makeup. And then she dressed in my clothes and took her place onstage without ever meeting anyone's eye. When the curtain rose, she filled with life. She sang and danced and kissed and fought. The audience cried, and during curtain call she blew kisses to the little girls in the front row. When the curtain fell, her shoulders stooped and she stood with her head bent forward into the heels of her hands. Mr. McFarland put his hand on her shoulder, but she slapped it away and left him standing by himself, breathing into his fingers. Then she hung my clothes back in the costume room and left without saying good-bye. She did the same thing the next night. And the next.

On the fourth day, she called me. "The viewing is tonight," she said. "Before the show. I can't go alone."

"What about your mom?" I asked.

"She can't handle it," she said. "She hasn't left her room since we found . . . since it happened." Her breath was slow and heavy over the phone. "Will you come or not?"

When I climbed into her car she held up her hand. "Don't ask me how I am," she said. "Because I'm fine. I'm perfectly, one hundred percent fine."

The room at the church was dim and small, the size of my bedroom. I stood behind Dilly in the doorway and looked in at two rows of folding chairs. They were empty except for a girl, a softer, paler version of Dilly who sat alone in the front row. On the other side of the room, a single light was cast down onto a white bassinet and I turned my head away when I realized what was inside.

"This is my sister," Dilly said to me. "This is Grace."

The sister looked at me with dead, empty eyes and I

wasn't sure what I was supposed to say. "You guys look a lot alike," I said.

"Nobody's here," the sister said to Dilly.

"Who would come?" Dilly asked. "We don't know any-body." The sister nodded, and Dilly sat down beside her. "Have a seat, Grace," she said. But I was afraid to lift my eyes off the carpet for a single second. I couldn't trust them. I knew where they would look.

"I can't stay long," Dilly said to her sister. "I have to get into makeup."

"No," the sister said. "No, you can't leave me here by myself." My knees and ankles were beginning to tremble and I touched the wall to steady myself.

"I don't have a choice," Dilly said quietly and put her hand on top of her sister's. "People are *counting* on me."

The sister's voice caught in her throat. "I'm counting on you," she said and started to cry. "Please don't leave me here by myself." The room was too hot, but I felt cold all over. I clenched my jaw to keep my teeth from chattering, but it pushed the chatter down into my stomach and shoulders so that my whole body flinched and shook.

Dilly pushed her sister's hair behind her ear with one hooked finger and touched her chin to her sister's shoulder. "I told you I wouldn't be able to stay," she said, and the sis-ter leaned forward to cry into her knees. Dilly stood up and twisted her hands in front of her. "I don't know what to do," she said. Then she looked at me. "Grace," she said.

"No," I said.

Dilly took my arm. "Grace, listen."

"No."

"Just for a little while. So she isn't alone."

I walked out into the hallway and Dilly followed me. "You

knew this," I said to her. "You knew you were going to do this the whole time."

"Grace," she said. "I have to be there. You know I have to be there." I couldn't stop the shaking. It was everywhere now, in my lips and eyelids, in the soles of my feet.

"I can't," I told her. "I won't know what to do."

"Jesus Christ, Grace. You don't have to *do* anything. You don't even have to talk. Just sit there." I shook my head. "You know I have to be there, Grace. You *know* it."

"So do I," I told her. "I have to be there too. I have a line."

Dilly hit her hand against the wall. "For fuck's sake, Grace, somebody else can call for the pastor!"

We didn't say much, the sister and I. She asked me how old I was and I told her. She asked me if I liked school and I said yes. I stared down at my lap and tried to think of reasons to leave. I couldn't call my parents. They were at the play.

A couple of people came, the sister's friends from when she was in school, and each time one did, I thought how I could get up and walk to the bus stop, how I could get back to school in time for the second act. In time to call for the pastor. But none of the friends stayed longer than a minute, and before I could get up the nerve to go, the sister and I were alone again. While I was staring at my hands, she stood up and walked over to the bassinet.

"Do you like her dress?" she asked me.

"Uh-huh," I said, even though I was looking down and couldn't see it.

"It's a christening dress," she said. "I think it's beautiful."

I pulled my knees up to my chest and wrapped my arms around them to keep from shivering.

"Would you like to hold her?"

"What?" I asked, and when I looked up, the sister was standing in front of me with her arms full of lace and white eyelet.

"Here," she said and held it out to me. My arms moved without my mind and I stared straight ahead without looking down. It felt like nothing. It smelled like nothing. I watched the wall in front of me. If I didn't look, it wasn't real. It was nothing.

By the time I got back to school, the play was over and everyone was gone. I stood in the darkened costume room and sifted through Dilly's wardrobe until I found a skirt and blouse belonging to me. I had to get out of my clothes. I had to get that wet, nothing smell away from me, off my body. The costume smelled like Dilly's sweat and perfume, like something mean and powerful, and inside it, I imagined that I could still feel the heat from her body. I looked at myself in the mirror. She would miss the clothes. But that was just too bad. They were mine, after all. I was allowed to take them back if I wanted to. And I did. I wanted to take back all the things that were mine.

I pulled all of my clothes off the hangers and piled them next to the door. There would be nothing left for her tomorrow night, I thought. She could wear a potato sack for all I cared. She could go naked.

I thought of my parents' sofa in the prop room. I wouldn't be able to get it home, but I could beat it up if I wanted to. I could rip it apart with scissors and pull out all the fluff. I could peel back the leather and hide it in the Dumpster outside. I couldn't take it back, but I could make it worthless.

The prop room was dark, but it wasn't empty. From the doorway, I could make out the silhouette of a person sitting on the sofa. "I knew you'd come back," Mr. McFarland said.

"You did?" I asked.

"Grace?" he said, and I nodded. "I'm sorry." His voice was dull and sleepy. "I thought you were . . . You're wearing her clothes."

"They're my clothes," I said. "I lent them to her."

"Why are you here?" he asked.

"Why are you?"

The air was warm and the room smelled safe, like sawdust and tempera paint. "I don't have anyplace else to be," he said. I could still see only his outline in the dark. He wasn't a real person. He was only the shape of one.

"Neither do I," I said and stepped closer to him.

"Has she said anything to you?" he asked.

I took another step forward. "She's fine."

"But she never says anything," he said. "Does she talk to you?"

I could make out a face now. The whiteness of his skin. The dark sockets of his eyes. I could feel him breathing. I could hear his heartbeat. "She never talks about *you*," I said.

I stood in front of him, close enough to smell his hair, to touch the toe of his shoe with mine. I could make him want me. I could make him love me. I could make him go crazy if he didn't get enough of me.

I slid my knee between his. "I held a dead baby tonight," I said, and his legs tightened around my leg. His breath was harder. His hands moved up my hips and closed around my waist. As I reached out to touch his hair, he closed his eyes and leaned his face forward into my chest, pulling me closer and exhaling into the fabric of my blouse. He tightened his grip and breathed open-mouthed into my clothing like he'd never tasted air. Like he'd spent his whole life hungry. And then I was underneath him, under the heat of him, under the weight of him, under the moment of him that belonged to me. He didn't kiss me. He didn't say my name. He didn't open his eyes until we were finished.

Nine

Tess lies sometimes. At school, she says that she has speech therapy on Tuesdays after social studies. She is careful to lisp when she says it—*thpeech therapy after thocial thtudieth*. Her teacher says that Tess is precocious, that she tells good stories. "What a good story!" Miss Morris says when Tess tells her that she is a hemophiliac and has to be extra careful about things like blisters and paper cuts. Her illness is genetic, Tess says. Her mother is also a hemophiliac.

Tess is eight years old. Lying is something she will probably outgrow. This is what Mrs. Stuart, who takes care of Tess after school, thinks. Tess says that the stars are lonely, that the walls are crying, that late at night the trees outside her window fill with breath and whisper the names of dead children. Mrs. Stuart touches her wrinkled hand to the side of Tess's face and clucks her tongue when she says, "That's just pretend."

But everything in Tess's world is pretend. In her bedroom, the dolls stare at the walls with their flat, sticker eyes, and the glass ballerina holds a perfect pose inside her tiny glass box. Beside the window, Tess's little table is set with empty teacups and a plate of plastic muffins. "Would you care for more tea?" Tess asks the nobody who sits across from her. She swallows cups of invisible tea. She chews mouthfuls of air.

Tess is a child, and like any child she has fears. She is afraid of sirens and lightning and words she doesn't understand (*eclectic, infinity, precocious*). She is afraid of falling off the earth. Some nights after dinner, she crawls through the house on her hands and knees, gripping the carpet with her fingernails. Her father says that she will not fall off the earth, that falling off the earth is impossible. Tess repeats the word slowly, tasting the slant and dip of each letter: *impossible*.

Tess's father is a grown-up. He understands with perfect clarity the things that can and cannot happen. He doesn't let himself be concerned that Tess cannot yet see the distinction. She is his only child, and he does not think of her as a liar. Instead, he believes that Tess is peculiar in the way that very intelligent people often are. He tries to find the humor in it. When Miss Morris calls from school to say that Tess has said her father is dying of lung cancer, he laughs. He assures Miss Morris that he isn't even a smoker (well, hardly), *that he is as right as rain*. Tess swings her legs against the bars of the kitchen chair as she listens to her father's end of the conversation. She does not understand. Right as rain. Miss Morris says that Tess is bright and sensitive and doing very well in geography. When he hangs up the phone, Tess's father pats her on the shoulder. "Everything's fine," he tells her. "Don't worry."

But Tess worries. She worries about fires and floods and poisonous-spider bites. In the car, she cranes her neck to see accidents on the freeway, to memorize details of broken glass and twisted metal. Drying dinner dishes, she holds the sharp kitchen knives and feels a tightening in her spine, a throbbing ache across the spidery blue veins in her wrists. When she walks to school in the morning, the older boys drive their cars too fast down the road, and Tess watches as they pass in a blur of noise and grit and cigarette smoke. She imagines herself pressed between them, imagines the way the air would smell of sweat and gasoline, and the wind would stir her hair into tangles. Day after day she stands beside the road in her glasses and ponytail, waiting for them to notice her, waiting for them to stop. *Want a piece of candy, little girl?*

In two weeks Tess will be nine. And after nearly nine years in this world, she knows that some things need to be worried about. Mrs. Stuart had a dog that got struck by lightning. A girl at Tess's school drowned in a swimming pool. Cars crashed. Knives slipped. Sometimes, women got into strange cars with strange men and didn't ever come back.

Tess's mother left two years ago, and her red raincoat is still hanging in the front closet. When Tess gets her own raincoat before school in the morning, she sees the red stripe of her mother's coat among her father's black wool, and her knees turn soft like clay. Not much that belongs to her mother is left in this house. Her mother took some things with her when she went away—clothes and jewelry, the painting of sand dunes that used to hang in the upstairs bathroom, the goldfish. Other things her father got rid of nearly a year later, while Tess was at school. "Your mother's moved forward," her father said when Tess came home to find the clean, flat squares her mother's things had left in the carpet, the blank spaces on the walls. "We should too."

Of course, he hadn't gotten everything. The leftover things were small, tiny sometimes: a hairpin in the crevice of a drawer, a string of seashells over a doorknob, a sliver of black soap in the bathtub. These things revealed themselves to Tess over time, sifting up through the countertop clutter or the shadows of a cabinet. She would look down one day, and there they would be: the hairpin, the seashells, the soap. Her mother had been there, and there, and there.

But the raincoat, that is something big. Tess thinks of all the afternoons she has spent watching television with Mrs. Stuart in the living room, all the times she's come through the front door or stood in the kitchen or brushed her teeth. For two whole years, the red raincoat has been hanging in the front closet like an open wound. And for two whole years, no one has said a word about it.

Tess walks to school with the rain making cold, fat plops on the hood of her jacket. She tries to look up at the sky, but the water stings her eyes, and she has to keep her head down. Maybe it doesn't rain in the place where her mother lives now. And even if it does, two years is a long time. Her mother must have bought a new raincoat by now.

At school, Miss Morris chooses people to act out the assassination of Lincoln. She tells the class how Lincoln studied by candlelight and ended slavery and always told the truth. "Honest Abe," they called him, because he could not tell a lie. Miss Morris says that after Lincoln was shot, they saved the bloody pillow he died on, and you can still go see it. "Of course, they keep it covered with plastic now," she says.

At Tess's school, they don't like guns or toys that look like guns, so the boy who plays John Wilkes Booth points his finger at the back of Lincoln's head and says, "Bang!" Von Maxwell, who is playing Lincoln, has taken a packet of ketchup from the cafeteria, and when John Wilkes Booth shoots him, he slaps the packet against the side of his head so that a little stream of ketchup burps onto the floor. "You got me!" he yells and drops sideways out of his chair. "I'm a goner now!"

Today is Tuesday, and after social studies Tess has to leave (*thpeech therapy*). But her lisp is only pretend, and she does not go to the speech therapist. Instead she goes to see Dirk and Deborah. Dirk and Deborah are new at the school this year. They have an office next to the janitor's closet, with kitten posters on the wall and little bags of animal crackers that they let Tess eat while they ask her questions about her mother or about what color she thinks her insides are. Dirk and Deborah keep felt puppets in their office that they try to make Tess talk to when she doesn't want to talk about her mother or her insides, which is always. Once a week Dirk and Deborah bring their puppets into Tess's classroom and put on shows to teach the children about things like not talking to strangers and what to do if you catch on fire.

Today, Tess tells Dirk and Deborah about Honest Abe and how they shot him and saved his bloody pillow. Dirk sits on his desk with his legs crossed Indian-style and asks if learning about the assassination made Tess sad, because she can tell them if it did. Or if it didn't, Deborah says, Tess can tell them that too. When Tess does not answer, Dirk and Deborah glance at each other, and Tess knows that she is going to have to give them something soon. She does not want to talk to the puppets. Last week, Dirk put a puppet on his arm and made Tess sing "Row, Row, Row Your Boat" in a round with him. He wouldn't shut up until she did it.

"My birthday's soon," Tess says. "Two weeks from now."

Dirk and Deborah's eyebrows lift, and their mouths open into happy gaping holes. This is wonderful news!

Tess shrugs. Certain ages are more important than others. Seven, for example, was an age you could really sink your teeth into, so much older than six. Ten would be the same—a whole new world. Nine is just one of the bald-headed numbers in between. Tess could take it or leave it.

Deborah writes the date down in her calendar. "We'll remember to bring you something special that day," she says.

The other kids in Tess's class do not like Dirk and Deborah. They call them "queers" and "retards" and shoot tiny balls of paper at their heads with rubber bands while they perform their puppet shows. Tess is always careful to keep her eyes on her desk, to not show that she knows Dirk and Deborah better than anyone else. But now, in their office, Tess imagines Deborah at the mall, picking out a night-light or a bracelet with Tess's name on it, then taking it home to wrap it in white paper and a pink bow. She feels like crying. "It's all right," she tells them. "You don't have to."

Deborah leans forward and squeezes Tess's knee. "It's okay to be happy about the good things," she says. "It's okay if something makes you feel like smiling."

Dirk nods. "Or if it doesn't," he says. "That's okay too."

After school, Tess watches *One Life to Live* with Mrs. Stuart. Nora is recovering from brain surgery alone in her beach house, and Todd Manning, who has been out for revenge ever since Nora sabotaged him during his trial for raping Marty last summer, is stalking her. Tess sucks on one of the butter-scotch Life Savers that Mrs. Stuart keeps in her purse, while Nora wanders through the beach house in her nightgown and neck bandage, stumbling into walls and tripping over furniture. Todd Manning is coming for her, waiting around every corner, hiding in every shadow. The lights have gone out, and Nora falls to the floor.

When the show is over, Mrs. Stuart goes into the kitchen to make dinner for Tess and her father, and to pack Tess's lunch for the next day. The television is off, and through the curtains, the light looks blue, as if the room were underwater. Tess closes her eyes and imagines blindness, entrapment, a loose bandage on her neck. As Mrs. Stuart chops vegetables in the kitchen, Tess thinks of her mother's raincoat hiding in the hall closet like a bloody stranger. When her father gets home from work, Tess will make him feel her head for tumors. She will make him check her bedroom closet for men with knives.

But when her father gets home, a woman is with him, and he says that he will feel Tess's head for tumors another time, when they don't have company. The woman's name is Meredith. She is tall and thin, with pale hair and so many freckles that, up close, her skin looks like the pink marble steps at the public library. Meredith stands in their kitchen with one hip cocked, swirling the red wine in her glass. "Your daughter has tumors?" she asks.

Tess's father coughs into the back of his wrist. "Oh," he says. "She's just being funny."

While Tess and her father eat, Meredith sits at the table, moving the food around her plate with her fork. Tess's father says that Meredith is a dancer with the city ballet and maybe they can go see her perform sometime. Won't that be fun?

Tess has been to the ballet before. When she was little, her mother took her into the city to see *The Nutcracker*. Tess wore a green velvet dress, and her mother carried her good purse. They sat together in the darkness, watching girls in white dresses twirl beneath fake snow. Tess fell asleep halfway through. She cannot remember if she had fun or not.

While her father clears the dinner dishes, Tess watches Meredith from across the table. Her sweater dips down into a V, and Tess can see the bones, like a ladder, on her speckled chest. Meredith lifts her wine to her lips, and the cuff of her sleeve falls away from her wrist, exposing a bone as small and perfect as a glass marble. "Are you anorexic?" Tess asks.

Meredith sets her wine back on the table without drinking. "Are you rude?" she asks.

"You can die from it," Tess says.

Meredith leans her chin into the cup of one freckled hand. "You're the expert."

Tess and Meredith watch each other across the table, and Tess feels a tickling in her spine as Meredith lifts one pale eyebrow into a perfect arch. They do not like each other. This will be their secret.

"I have low blood sugar," Tess says. "If I don't eat, I faint."

"Wow," Meredith says.

"Sometimes I throw up," Tess adds. "While I'm fainted."

Tess's father makes a pot of coffee, and he and Meredith sit at the table smoking cigarettes. Tess stands behind her chair, and her father pinches her on the ribs to make her laugh. When she goes to kiss him good night, she can smell wine and cigarette smoke on his lips. In times past, Tess would wrap her arms around her father's neck to kiss him, but now she only touches her mouth to his—not a real kiss, but something that looks like one. Tess knows that even these pretend kisses will stop soon. She will be nine, then ten, then eleven. Soon she will be too old to tickle. And then they will not touch at all.

Tess says good night, then stands outside the door, listening.

"She's adorable," Meredith says.

"Thank you," Tess's father says.

"What happened to her mother?"

At night, Tess's bedroom fills with shadows, and the trees tap secret messages on her window. Her dolls think only of themselves—their yarn hair and dead eyes. On her dresser the little ballerina holds perfectly still, her toes pointed, her arms lifted, reaching up toward her glass sky. No one sees Tess cry. And so it doesn't count.

Tess begins crying for a number of reasons. Tonight, she thinks about Mrs. Stuart's dog, the one that was struck by lightning. Tess did not know the dog; she has only heard stories about him. He was Mrs. Stuart's dog when she was a little girl, and before he was struck by lightning, he slept in Mrs. Stuart's bed, with her. Mrs. Stuart has told Tess that the dog smelled like wet grass and made low, doggy snores in his sleep. Tess cries for the dog who died, and for Mrs. Stuart who missed him, and for herself, a girl who has never had a dog.

Much later, Tess hears noises in the hallway—her father and Meredith, their voices low and thick with laughter. "I love you, I love you, I love you," her father's voice says through the wall.

Love. It is a word that means nothing and everything at

the same time. When Tess was little, her mother used to cry in the bathtub. All the time. Tess would creep into the bathroom and kneel beside the tub, while her mother held the black egg of soap in her hands and wept into her knees. "I love you," Tess would tell her. "I love you, I love you." And her mother would cry and stroke Tess's hair into cords of gray lather.

"I'm so sorry," her mother would say, hiccuping. "I start crying, and I just can't stop."

Hemophilia is when something gets started and then can't stop. Tess learned all about this from *One Life to Live*. It exists in families, mothers passing the sickness down to their babies so that wounds, once open, can never be closed. People die from it.

"I love you, I love you," her father's voice says on the other side of the wall, and Tess wants to rush to him and cover his lips with her hand. She wants to save him from all the things he hopes it means, from all the promises it cannot keep.

Instead, she presses her face into her pillow and thinks about having something all her own to love—something small and furry that she could kiss and name and touch with her hands. In Tess's classroom, they have hamsters: a girl hamster named Marigold, and a boy hamster named Bon Jovi. Once, they had baby hamsters, pink and hairless like a pile of squirming thumbs. Miss Morris said that when the hamsters got bigger, she would give them to the students who knew their state capitals best, that those students would each be able to take a baby hamster home to keep. Every day after school, Tess sat at her little table and wrote the capitals over and over again, until the words became part of herself, as real and familiar as her own name. She would have gotten a perfect score except that she mixed up the Virginias. But in the end, Bon Jovi ate all the baby hamsters, and nobody got to have one.

In the next four days, Meredith spends the night twice. The first time, she is gone when Tess wakes up. The second time, Tess goes to brush her teeth in the morning and finds her in the bathroom. Meredith is standing at the sink in her tank top and underpants, holding her hair off her pink-speckled shoulders and making kissy faces at herself in the mirror. When she sees Tess in the doorway, she jumps.

"Morning," she says as Tess reaches across her for the toothbrush. "Want me to leave?"

Tess stares at Meredith in the mirror, her long corded neck and smeared eye makeup. Yes, she wants Meredith to leave. She wants her to take her cigarettes and her perfect posture and never come back. But this is not what Meredith means.

Tess squeezes a glob of toothpaste onto her brush and scrubs until her gums burn and the foam inside her mouth turns pink with blood. Meredith shifts her weight from one foot to the other, staring at her own reflection instead of at Tess. "I could fix your hair for you if you want," she says after Tess rinses and spits into the sink.

"My mom used to do that," Tess says. "Before she died."

Meredith meets Tess's eye in the mirror. "Your mom isn't dead."

"How do you know?" Tess asks.

"Your dad told me."

The bathroom is not cold, but Tess's teeth begin to chatter. Her ankles wobble. She holds her head with both hands and crumples onto the floor.

Meredith jumps sideways. "Jesus," she says. "Are you all right?"

"It's my blood," Tess says. "My sugar is low."

"Should I get your dad?" Meredith asks.

Tess waves at her face with one open hand and peers up at Meredith through the slits of her eyelids. "Food," she whispers, and Meredith runs into the hall. When she comes back, she has a glass of juice and a slice of plain wheat bread. Meredith has not poured the juice into a juice glass, but into a regular glass. Tess begins to point this out, then decides that a person in her weakened condition should not be bothered with such details.

Meredith sits on the floor while Tess sips her juice and takes little nibbles of bread. "Feeling better?" she asks, and Tess nods.

Meredith pulls her knees to her chest, circling them with her spindly arms as she watches Tess eat.

"My mom *might* be dead," Tess says.

Meredith tilts her head. "You shouldn't say that."

"She was sick," Tess says.

"I'm sorry," Meredith says. "Your dad didn't tell me that."

Tess does not have to look at the bathtub to know that the sliver of black soap is still curled in the corner of the soap dish. Two years have passed, and no one has thrown it away. "Maybe he didn't know."

At school, Tess's class watches a puppet show on how to know if your parents are abusing you. It's about Billy and Billy's mom. In the story, the Billy puppet realizes that the Billy's-mom puppet is abusing him. He sings a song about it, and afterward Dirk and Deborah teach the song to the class so that they can all sing it together while Deborah plays the guitar.

Von Maxwell leans over from the desk beside Tess's and holds his face close to hers so that she can smell the chocolate cake from lunch souring on his breath. "You're ugly," he whispers and sticks her arm with the point of his pencil. "You have big, ugly ears."

Tess's ears prickle. They are pink and naked at the sides of her head like two cupped hands sticking out through her hair. She stares straight ahead at the Billy puppet, at his flat, lipless mouth and blank circle eyes. It is the same puppet that played Andy last week in a show about how to know if your friends are selling drugs.

When the song is finished, Deborah asks if anyone has a question. Beth, whose mouth is always wet and spitty in the corners, raises her hand. "Does Billy's mom ever hit him with a rolled-up newspaper?" she asks.

Dirk frowns. "Mmm, maybe," he says. "But mostly she does really *bad* things, like hold his hand on a hot stove."

Dirk and Deborah pack up their puppets and squeeze between the rows of desks on their way to the back of the classroom. As they pass, Deborah winks at Tess and gives her the thumbs-up sign.

"What's with that?" Von asks.

Tess stares down at her hands. "Who knows?" she says. "They're such retards."

Tess is going to be nine soon. This is the way her father begins the conversation. Tess can tell that it is going to be a serious conversation, because her father asks her to sit at the kitchen table with him, and mealtime is hours away. Tess's father says that an active imagination is a wonderful thing to have. But you have to know the difference between what is imaginary and what is not. "Do you understand about truth?" he asks.

Tess looks into his face and tries to think what the right answer might be.

"Your mother," he says and taps his fingers lightly on the tabletop. "She isn't dead. She isn't sick. She's just gone." He holds up the palms of his empty hands to show her—*gone*. "Do you understand?"

Tess understands that she sometimes tells lies. She does. But they are little, unimportant lies. Sick. Dead. Gone. What do her lies matter to anyone else? Why does the world care?

Her father reaches across the table and squeezes Tess's fingers in his. "Some things are real, and some things aren't," he says. "Part of getting older is learning to understand the difference. Okay?"

Tess's head feels heavy on her neck. Her brain is smooth and shiny like plastic. Her blood is ketchup. She could hold her own hand against a hot stove and not feel a thing. "Okay," she says.

The morning of Tess's birthday, she stands in front of the mirror in her pajamas. She is exactly the same as she was yesterday—big-eared.

When she passes her father's bedroom, she can make out the shape of Meredith's body pressed against his in the bed. Her father sleeps with one leg thrown across Meredith at the hip, his face buried in the tangles of her hair.

Downstairs in the refrigerator, she finds a rectangular box wrapped in balloon paper—a present from Mrs. Stuart.

Tess opens the package on the kitchen table and takes a step backward. It is a lunch box, bright red, with a picture of Raggedy Ann riding a bicycle. Raggedy Ann is smiling wide with her pink cartoon lips and black cartoon eyes. The sky is blue. The sun is shining.

Tess can't express what will be done to her if she shows up at school carrying this lunch box. No one will kick a girl. No one will hit her or push her or throw a clump of mud at her head. But they will laugh at her. They will stare. They will stand to the side and watch her be alone.

When she goes to the hall closet for her raincoat, the stripe of red stops her. She pictures her father's square hands, open and empty—*just gone.* She slides her mother's coat off the hanger, thinking it might smell like soap or perfume. But when she sniffs at the cuffs and collar, nothing of her mother remains. The coat smells like the closet. The hem falls to Tess's ankles, and she has to roll up the sleeves, but as she looks at herself in the hallway mirror, she thinks that the coat does not look so wrong on her. It might have belonged to her the whole time. She walks through the front door in the red coat, leaving the child's lunch box on the kitchen table.

At school, no one knows that today is Tess's birthday. She has not brought cupcakes or cookies. She is not wearing a new dress. During craft time, the children in her class make silhouettes of Lincoln's head out of black construction paper, then glue the black paper heads onto white paper. The work isn't hard, just tracing, but somehow Tess's head looks more like a duck than like a president, and she has to stay inside during morning recess to do it over.

"If you'd drawn somebody like Jefferson or Washington,"

Miss Morris says, "I wouldn't care so much about you redoing it. But Lincoln was a really important president."

Tess is nearly finished with her second Lincoln head when Dirk and Deborah come through the classroom door with their guitar cases and puppet bags. They are wearing headbands with fuzzy pink balls attached to spring antennae. Tess looks over her shoulder at them. They are not supposed to be here today. Deborah holds her arms out from her sides. "There's the birthday girl!" she cries, and Tess's whole body goes dead.

"Are you here to do a show?" she asks.

"A special one," Dirk tells her. "Just for you."

The recess bell rings, and Tess can hear feet pounding toward the building. Her mind spins in circles, searching for an answer. The nurse's office. She needs to be sick. She needs to be injured. She looks down at the scissors and thinks about jamming them into her leg, but they are schoolroom scissors, short and fat with round, plastic tips. Useless. Dirk and Deborah pile their bags on a table at the front of the room and begin to unpack their puppets as Tess's classmates tumble through the back door in a noisy, muddy stew.

As a last resort, Tess turns to God. She does not go to church, does not pray before bed or meals or spelling tests. But she prays now. She prays to burn with a fever or shake with a deep, phlegmy cough. She knows that girls can make themselves throw up (she saw a puppet show once), but she is not clear on the technique, and as she wills her stomach to turn and seize, she knows that this hoping is fruitless. She is not sick. She is not dying. God hates her.

And then, maybe for the first time since she was born, God looks down from heaven and sees her. She can feel the moment, the exact instant when God knows that she is there, that she needs help. Tess looks over her shoulder and there, standing in the doorway, is Meredith. She holds up the Raggedy Ann lunch box. "You forgot this," she mouths, and Tess knocks her chair over as she runs to the back of the room. By the time she reaches Meredith, she is already crying.

Meredith squats down. "What?" she asks. "What's happened?"

Tess points to the front of the classroom, where Dirk is untangling felt limbs, his pink antennae bobbing above his head like two wads of cotton candy. "Those puppets are gonna sing to me," she gasps between hiccups. She prays that Meredith will understand, that she will hear the words Tess cannot find.

Meredith looks over Tess's head at the front of the classroom, then at Miss Morris, who is helping Beth unjam the zipper of her jacket. "Grab your coat," she says. The rest of Tess's classmates are slipping out of their muddy shoes and making their way to their desks. No one sees Tess and Meredith leave.

In the car, Tess pulls her knees to her chest and cries until she thinks she is going to break. "Maybe you need to eat something," Meredith suggests and cracks her window to light a cigarette. This is not exactly convenient for Meredith—she says so several times while Tess is crying into her knees. She doesn't have time to take Tess all the way back home. Tess will have to come along.

Tess turns her face sideways. "To the ballet?" she asks.

"To the rehearsal," Meredith says.

But Tess does not want to go anywhere. She closes her

eyes and waits for the world to disappear from the inside out, to swallow itself inside her and go away forever.

"So," Meredith says after a minute, "do puppets sing to you a lot?"

Tess opens her eyes, and they are still driving, the windshield wipers beating against a backdrop of drab sky. "Today is my birthday," she says.

Meredith winces. "Oh God, I totally forgot," she says. "Happy birthday."

"Thanks," Tess sniffs.

Meredith exhales a silvery stream of smoke through the slit at the top of the window. "Did you get anything cool?" she asks.

Tess looks down at the Raggedy Ann lunch box on her lap, and her face spasms into a fresh wave of tears, her shoulders heaving.

"Oh no." Meredith covers her mouth with her hand as she starts to laugh. "I'm not laughing," she says.

"It's from Mrs. Stuart," Tess says.

"Well, it's truly awful," Meredith says. "Relax, though. Your dad got you some good stuff."

"Did he get me a dog?" Tess asks.

Meredith flicks the end of her cigarette out into the rain and rolls up her window. "No."

Tess traces her finger around the edge of the lunch box. At one time she would have carried it without a thought, back when her shoes had Velcro straps and her mother put her hair in braids before she left for school. Back then, Tess could accept blue skies and bright suns and cartoon worlds where she could expect nothing but happiness. She cannot remember who she was then. "Sometimes," she says, "I start crying and I can't stop."

Meredith glances sideways at her. "Well," she says after a minute. "Welcome to the wonderful world of womanhood."

They pull into a gas station, and Meredith hands Tess a quarter. "Call your father at work," she says. "Explain."

Tess crosses the parking lot to the phone booth, the rain soaking the back of her neck. Inside, she slips Meredith's quarter into the slot and dials the number. The phone rings, and Tess thinks about what she will say to explain. Dirk and Deborah were wearing headbands, they brought guitars. Of all the things that had ever happened, *this* was the thing Tess would not have been able to survive. It would have killed her.

But these are all the wrong words. Her father will not understand. He will say that the puppet show would not have killed her, that she was being impossible. He will tell her to go back to school. "Good morning," her father's voice says, and Tess clicks the grimy receiver back onto its hook.

"Copacetic?" Meredith asks when Tess climbs back into the car.

"Everything's fine," Tess tells her and blows a chilly circle of fog onto the window. "Don't worry."

Watching Meredith's ballet, Tess sees no white dresses, no toys that come to life underneath fake snow. Instead, she sees women with spines that move like ribbons of knucklebones beneath their sweat-soaked leotards, and a short, barrel-chested man with a bald head like Daddy Warbucks who yells for them to do it *higher! Faster! Better!*

Tess sits with her back against the wall, and the floor trembles beneath her as the dancers leap and twirl, their feet pounding again and again. Up close, nothing about it is pretty. The dancers' faces are splotched with red, the cords of their

43

necks are hard and throbbing, their hair is darkening with sweat as they rise and land, punishing their pink-slippered feet against the dusty floor. When one of the dancers stumbles, Daddy Warbucks shouts that she is a worthless waste of bone and cartilage and would be better off spending her time looking for a husband. The woman's face cracks as he yells, tears spilling over the rims of her eyes and down her sweaty cheeks. But she doesn't cover her face or run from the room. She keeps dancing.

Afterward, Tess sits in the locker room, nibbling at the sandwich from her Raggedy Ann lunch box, while Meredith and the other dancers peel off their ballet slippers and leotards. Their feet are cracked and swollen, with open blisters and shiny pink calluses, and they wince as they massage their heels and ankles. Tess's heart flutters in her throat as she watches. Regular people see only the finished show, with lights and costumes and music so loud that it covers the sounds of feet striking the floor. But Tess has seen the ugly truth: blood and bruises and sweat. She is special.

"What did you think?" Meredith asks in the car.

Tess sits on the edge of her seat, electricity coursing through her veins and muscles. Where to begin? "I want to be a dancer."

Meredith gives her a sideways glance, and for a moment she looks pleased. But then her face screws up, and she turns her eyes back to the road. "You're a little old," she says. "Most people start when they're itty-bitty."

All of the air seems to suck itself from Tess's lungs. She will never be a dancer, insect-thin, with bloody, aching feet. She is nine years old. She has wasted her life. But then she thinks of Honest Abe, how he was poor and lonely, how he studied by candlelight. "I would practice really hard," she says.

Meredith smiles. "I know some people who give classes," she says. "I could make some calls, if it's really what you want."

Tess can feel the thoughts spinning inside Meredith's head—if Tess takes ballet classes, they will have something in common, something they can talk about while they move their food around their plates at dinnertime. They will speak the same language. Meredith will give Tess tights and toe shoes and fix her hair before school. She will marry Tess's father. She will stay forever.

"It is," Tess says. "It's what I want."

They pull up to the house and see two police cars in the driveway. The front door is open, and Mrs. Stuart is crying on the porch. Meredith sinks back against the seat as she looks up at the house. "Oh *shit*," she whispers. The policemen are running toward the car, Tess's father behind them. Tess and Meredith get out of the car, and everyone begins yelling.

The phys-ed teacher was out fixing a tetherball when she saw Tess get into a car with a woman. She told the police that Tess seemed to know the woman, that Tess looked like she was crying. One of the policemen is holding Tess's school picture. The other is holding a picture of her mother.

The police yell at Meredith, and Meredith yells back. Tess's father walks toward Meredith, and for a second, Tess thinks he might hit her. Instead, he reaches out, pushing Meredith with both hands so that she stumbles and her head snaps back on the string of her neck. Tess's father stands over Meredith and drops his arms to his sides, balling his hands into fists. His face is white, his mouth wrenching back in the corners when he yells, "What the hell were you thinking? What the hell's *wrong* with you?"

Meredith is shaking, her mouth opening and closing in soundless gasps. She looks up at Tess's father through the narrow slits of her eyes, and the policemen step between them. "You called, right?" Meredith asks Tess. The rain is falling in sheets, flattening Meredith's hair against her skull and streaking her face so that Tess cannot tell if she is crying. "You explained?"

Everyone looks at Tess, and she stands in the middle, trying to explain. Meredith is breathing hard. Her father's hair is messy. Mrs. Stuart stands behind Tess with her hands on Tess's shoulders, leaning forward to cry onto the top of her head. The policemen twitch their mustaches, while Tess explains about Dirk and Deborah, about the forgotten lunch box and the felt puppets and God suddenly caring that she was alive and sending Meredith to save her. When she says this last part, her father closes his eyes, and Meredith stares down at her feet, rotating the toe of one shoe in the soggy grass.

It was all a misunderstanding, this is what the policemen say. No crime has been committed. No harm has been done. They clap Tess's father on the shoulder and tell him to get a stiff drink and a good night's sleep. As they leave, one looks seriously at Meredith. "For future reference," he tells her, "you can't just take somebody else's kid out of school."

"For future reference," Meredith says, "don't worry."

Mrs. Stuart leaves after the policemen, and then just the three of them are left. They stand on the front lawn, the rain pelting down on their heads and shoulders. "Well," Meredith says after a moment. "I guess I ought to go."

Tess's father lifts his head and takes a step toward Meredith, but she steps backward, massaging her neck with the heel of one hand. "We have a cake," her father says, and Meredith laughs without smiling, then turns toward her car. Tess looks at her father, waiting for him to stop her. But he stares down at the grass and says nothing.

Tess runs across the lawn after Meredith, reaching for the cuff of her sweater. "You could come inside for a minute," she says. "You could have a slice of birthday cake." Again, Tess's father lifts his head to look at Meredith, and again, she looks away.

Tess wants to remind Meredith about the ballet classes, the phone call she has promised to make, the new life that they will all live together. But before Tess can find the words, Meredith takes a breath. "Look," she says, holding her arms out to her sides. "I'm just a chorus dancer. It's not like I'm anybody cool."

Tess stands on the front lawn watching as Meredith climbs into her car and shuts the door. And then she is gone.

The lights are on inside the house, the windows glowing like squares of sunshine. In the kitchen, Tess sees a birthday cake, presents—the good stuff Meredith said Tess's father got for her. But they do not go inside. Tess's father sits on the porch steps, and she sits beside him, the rain soaking through the raincoat, dampening the seat of her jeans as the sky darkens above them. The pictures rest on her father's lap—the one they took of Tess at school, the one of her mother. In the picture, her mother is wearing a pink headband that Tess does not remember. She is smiling. "Where did you find that?" Tess asks.

He reaches one hand toward Tess's, his fingers hovering over the cuff of the red raincoat. And in that moment, Tess can feel all the answers welling up behind his lips, all the truths she's been waiting to be told. But then he pulls his arm back, turning the picture over on his lap so that her mother's smile disappears, and Tess sees only a blank white square. "Look at the rain," he says, and Tess looks. "You were born on a night just like this one."

Tomorrow, Tess's birthday will be over. She will get dressed and go to school. Mrs. Stuart will cook dinner, and Tess and her father will eat it. Today will just be something else that they don't talk about, something else that probably never happened.

Economics

That was the year I thought I'd never be happy again. I was eighteen and starting college at the school where my older sister was majoring in business—a small, pretty campus full of tall, pretty people, all of whom seemed easy and relaxed, as though they wanted nothing more than to live in this town and attend this college. I did not want to go to college, did not want to live with my sister, did not want to be an eleven-hour drive from my boyfriend, who, I knew, was not in love with me the way that I was in love with him and would quickly abandon the idea of me without the actual me around to keep him distracted with blowjobs. But my mother said I didn't have a choice about going to college, and I was still young enough to believe that because she said so, it was true.

For the past two years, my sister had been sharing her apartment with Betty, a fellow economics major she'd met at the Mexican restaurant where they both worked as waitresses. The Mexican restaurant was owned by a German couple, but it was in the hip part of town and hired only very attractive girls to work as waitresses, so a lot of people ate there even though the service was slow and the food was shitty. My sister said that it had been love at first sight with her and Betty, that during the time they'd spent living and working together, they had grown closer than friends. Closer than sisters.

Too bad, my mother said. She was paying for two college tuitions, and she was not going to pay for two apartments and two cars as well. I was coming: Betty would have to go.

Though Betty officially moved out, she still spent most of her time at our apartment, crying on our sofa and eating our cereal. Betty's boyfriend, my sister explained, was a real dick-hole, and Betty needed a lot of support. "I know it isn't your fault," Betty said the night I moved in. "It just really sucks that you're here."

When I wasn't in class, I spent most of my time in my room, waiting for my own boyfriend to call, which he did less and less, then not at all.

"You don't know how lucky you have it," my sister told me. "A lot of people would kill to live in Raingate."

The Raingate Village Apartment Complex was close to campus and had tennis courts and a swimming pool and a gym, which was really just one of the apartments with some hand weights and a couple of stationary bikes inside. The complex was filled with college students, people my sister knew from this class or that class or because they drank margaritas in the restaurant where she worked with Betty. Everyone had clear skin and suntans and smooth, muscular bodies they seemed to fill with nothing but Chinese food and cheap beer.

Betty's new apartment, she would have me know, was in Meadow Dwellings: a shitbox with no pool.

On the weekends, the residents of Raingate Village threw cookouts and parties by the pool, and my sister and Betty would pack beer into coolers, then stand in the doorway of my bedroom in their bikinis and flip-flops. "Come down," they always said, and I would say that I might later, though we all knew I was lying.

Alone in the apartment, I watched my sister's TV and smoked her pot and ate the food I thought she would be least likely to miss—canned beans and frozen corn, instant oatmeal that I mixed with water and ate cold. In the evenings, I sat on the balcony and smoked cigarettes, watching people come and go on the sidewalk below, looking for someone I could imagine myself falling in love with. The boys were all narrow-hipped and broad-shouldered, wearing baseball hats and T-shirts advertising sports teams and brands of beer. They referred to one another as *dudes* and *motherfuckers* and occasionally slammed their chests together to emphasize their brotherly bond.

Sometimes I tried to picture myself kissing one of these boys or lying naked with one of them in bed, and then I would picture myself committing suicide.

Am I exaggerating?

I'm mostly exaggerating.

In late September, the weather turned damp and chilly, and my sister said that it was time for me to get a job. She and Betty were looking at a very hectic semester—in addition to their waitress jobs and regular course schedules, they had both enrolled in Entrepreneurship in Modern America, a required class for economics majors and one that was famous, they told me, for giving people nervous breakdowns. The class was divided into five groups, and final grades were assigned according to how well each group managed to design, produce, market, and distribute whatever commodity the class agreed on. At the end of the semester, the group that made the largest profit would receive an A, the next a B, and so on.

This semester, the class had voted to make paper hats. My sister and Betty had their work cut out for them if theirs was to be the most successful paper hat business, so they were going to have to take fewer shifts at the Mexican restaurant. This meant less money for groceries and pot. If I intended to go on as I had, eating and smoking, I was going to have to make a financial contribution. Our goal as a household, my sister told me, was to be allocatively efficient.

Prairie Arts: A Boutique of Fine Gifts was close enough to the Mexican restaurant that my sister and I could share a car to work, but far enough away to no longer be in the same neighborhood. Sandwiched between a photocopy shop and a law office, Prairie Arts advertised itself as both gallery and supplier of all fine things this town had to offer: locally made art and jewelry, handcrafted keepsakes, postcards picturing surrounding rivers and the reservoir up in the mountains, and all types of clothing bearing the name and/or mascot of the college.

The store was owned by Richard Lutz, who went by Red because his son, whom I would never meet in the four or so months before I got fired, went by Richard. Red was, himself, a rare sight around the store, as he traveled for his other business, which had something to do with cellular phones sold in mall kiosks. During my interview Red explained that should I get the job, I would be working mostly for his daughter.

Amy Lutz, Red told me, was an honest-to-god prodigy. The first in the Lutz family to attend college, Amy was twenty years old and going full-time—a double major in business and communications with a minor in mathematics. And on top of that, she was managing Prairie Arts nearly single-handedly. A whole store! All by herself! With Amy's brains, Red said, she would be running a company someday.

Red gave me a tour of the store, which was empty aside from us. Prairie Arts had been in business for nearly eight years, and though they weren't all good years, Red thought things were looking up for the place. He'd started the store because of his sister—she made fudge and got tired of giving it away, but had no place to sell it. Red figured there must be other folks with this predicament, crafty folks who needed a spot to make a sale.

I looked around at the mugs and refrigerator magnets, the paintings of cowboys, the picture frames made out of sea-shells. "All this is local?" I asked, and Red waved one hand above his head. "More or less."

The key to the store's success, he told me, pointing to the front door, then to the back, was walk-throughs. "People can cross," he said, stabbing his finger again in the direction of the front door, "one street to the other without having to round the corner."

On the sidewalk outside, a woman with a stroller paused to squint into the front window. Red poked my arm with his elbow and gave me a knowing smile. "They take a shortcut, get it?" he whispered. "And maybe they see something they like."

We watched as the woman smiled into the window, then rubbed her front tooth with the pad of her index finger, straightened her skirt, and walked on. "Maybe they tell their friends," I added.

Red offered me the job right there on the spot because he

thought I was a bright girl and a fast learner, and I accepted because I thought it would be boring and easy.

The most important part of my job, Amy told me on my first day, was making sure that the cash drawer balanced. At the beginning and the end of every shift, I was to count the contents of the register—cash, checks, and credit card receipts—then check my final number against a master number that printed out on the register tape. If the two numbers didn't match up, I was to count the drawer again until they did. "Do it fifty times if you have to," she said. "The drawer has to balance."

Amy was thin and angular, with light eyes and a sharp, beaky nose. Her strawberry blond hair was nearly the same shade as her complexion so that, from a distance, she gave the eerie illusion of being all one color. Amy blinked rapidly as she explained the drawer-balancing procedure, her hands fluttering around the register without ever coming to rest on it.

"Do you think you can handle it?" she asked, and I told her that I thought I could since it was basically just counting and even monkeys could count. I said this as a joke, but I guess Amy didn't take it that way because she told me that some people have learning disabilities or other problems that make it very difficult for them to handle money. And also, in addition to making sure the drawer balanced, another important part of my job was vacuuming.

Most of my shifts passed without a single customer entering the store. When I arrived at work, I would count the drawer and check my number against the master. The numbers didn't always match, but I was never off by more than a few cents, a problem I solved by either adding the missing change from my own purse or removing the extra change from the drawer, slipping the coins into my pocket or hiding them behind the display of key chains. It wasn't like stealing. In the end, I figured, it would probably even out.

After I counted the drawer, I would do my homework, then wander around the store, dusting china figurines and arranging boxes of fudge into decorative stacks by the cash register. Amy spent most of her time in the back office, talking on the phone with her boyfriend or agonizing over her homework. Amy was also enrolled in Entrepreneurship in Modern America, and like my sister and Betty, she spent a great deal of time researching designs for paper hats and brainstorming marketing techniques.

Occasionally, someone came in from the street, and then I would try to hide the surprise in my voice as I asked if they were looking for something particular.

Our customers were usually out-of-towners—parents visiting their kids at college, or alumni returning to see what the place looked like after all these years. The people who liked Prairie Arts *really* liked Prairie Arts, and they spent hundreds of dollars at a time on souvenirs and gifts—mugs painted with the state flower, framed pictures of the mountains and the reservoir and the Historic Old Maine building on campus— and liked to tell me, as they shopped, about the differences between this town and the town where they lived: This town was hotter or less hot, drier or less dry. People here were so much nicer.

"Your job sounds like hell," said Betty, and my sister agreed.

At night they came home from the Mexican restaurant smelling like grease and sweat, and I would sit with them, watching late-night television and folding paper hats until my hands were black with newspaper ink. Other groups were making fancier hats, they told me, creative hats cut from colored paper and decorated with feathers or stickers or lottery tickets. But their group had opted to go in a different direction. Their strategy was simple: make the cheapest product, then sell a lot of it.

While we folded, they would tell me how they cared about me and were concerned for my future. What I needed, they said, was a real job, one for which I had to dress up and fix my hair and put on makeup.

But Prairie Arts had its perks. As long as the drawer balanced, Amy Lutz didn't really care what I did, and with so few customers, I could spend most of my time alone, which was how I preferred to spend my time. Also, the lawyers next door sometimes smoked me out on my breaks, and their pot was much better than anything anyone was smoking in Raingate Village.

"Are you high?" Amy asked when she came out of the office and found me sitting cross-legged on the jewelry counter, staring at a sculpture of an elk that had been carved from a tree stump.

Lying seemed like too much work so I told her that I was, a little.

She crossed her arms and looked down at the floor, pursing her mouth into a sideways pucker as she thought. "I guess it's all right," she said finally. "But it wouldn't be with my dad. It would be really, really *not* all right with my dad."

"Okay," I said. "I won't tell him."

It turned out that there was a whole range of things that would upset Red Lutz should he ever find out about them, the least of which seemed to be the drawer not balancing or me being high. The more I learned about Amy, the more I learned about the things that would not be all right with her father: Red would not be all right with Amy drinking and smoking, which did not keep her from doing either but created enough guilt and anxiety to prevent her from enjoying both. He would also not be all right with the fact that Amy hated Prairie Arts and sometimes fantasized about setting it on fire. Mostly, though, Red would not be all right with Hank.

Hank was a forty-five-year-old bartender, and Amy had been dating him for almost three months. She had not meant to fall for Hank the way she had, but now that she had, she lived a life of torment, consumed by distraction. All she could think about, she told me, was Hank. All day long, his image played like a movie in her head. This was a problem because of school, which required her full attention. It was also a problem because of her father, who, she said, would not approve of her relationship with Hank and might, if he ever found out about it, do something crazy like kill her.

I had not expected to like Hank because he was old and a bartender, and the idea of a girl my own age being in love with such a person frightened me. But one night Hank and Amy drove me home after work. When we pulled into Raingate Village, Hank turned around in his seat. "Hey," he said, "you live in Date Rape Village?" and then I couldn't help but like him a little.

Amy hated lying to her father, but I didn't really have a problem with it, so this became another important part of my job. If Red called and Amy was out with Hank, I would say that she was someplace else—the library, a study group, a showing of a documentary about the global cycles of supply and demand. At first I tried to keep the stories simple, but Red was enthralled with details and I sometimes couldn't help but elaborate.

"A documentary?" he asked. "She has to watch that for school? For a grade?"

"No," I told him, "she just wanted to see it because she thought it sounded interesting," and this struck such awe in him that for a moment, he was speechless.

Every few weeks, Red would come into the store and then I would lie to him in person: Amy wished she could spend more time at Prairie Arts, but she was working very hard on a big project for school. Her whole group was counting on her.

Red shook his head at the floor. It meant a lot to him, he said, me telling him all this. Amy still lived at home, but they didn't talk much.

"She might even make the dean's list this semester," I added, and he held one hand to his heart, his mouth opening and closing soundlessly as if it were simply too much to comprehend. Then he gave me twenty dollars and told me to take my boyfriend out for cheeseburgers.

A few nights later, Amy was counting the drawer when, suddenly, she began to cry.

"I'm seventy-five cents over," she said. Her back was curved, her shoulders heaving. "I can't find where I'm off."

"I'll fix it," I told her.

Amy gripped the cash drawer with both hands, her knuckles white as stones. The problem, she said, was not with the drawer, but with her life. She was flunking out of college. One more failing grade and that was that. She had been working as hard as she could, had thought she might be able to pull the semester off. But because of this one class, she would not.

She went back into the office and returned with a lump of something in her hands. The lump looked like a paper grocery bag spackled with glitter and sequins. She told me she'd been working on the paper hat for three hours—three hours!—and after all that time, she still couldn't make it stay on her head. Then she tore the hat in half and threw it on the floor.

Amy turned and lifted herself up on the sales counter, folding her legs beneath her and dabbing her eyes with the cuffs of her sweater before helping herself to a box of fudge.

She didn't know why, she said, but school had always come harder for her than it had for other people. Maybe she just wasn't as smart.

I said I thought she was pretty smart, and Amy peeled a piece of wax paper off a square of fudge, then dropped the candy neatly into her mouth.

The only thing that had ever felt easy to her, she said, was Hank. When Amy was with Hank, she didn't worry about sounding stupid or looking ugly. She had spent her whole life working as hard as she could to make a place for herself. But what she hadn't known was that her place was really a person. Until she met Hank, Amy told me, she had thought she would be lonely forever.

She ate another piece of fudge, then held the box out, offering me some.

No one got everything they wanted, Amy said, nodding in agreement with herself. But she had found a person who made her feel safe and pretty and peaceful, and wasn't that more than a lot of people had?

I told her it was.

Amy hopped off the counter, sweeping the fudge wrappers into the trash and dropping the ruined paper hat in after them. Then she told me that she was glad we'd had this talk, that I was around, and that we were friends.

I turned back to the register, pretending to recount the drawer. When I heard Amy round the corner behind me, I slid three quarters from the till, dropping them into the trash can, where they fell through the crumpled paper hat and the fudge wrappers and clattered at the bottom like a handful of rocks.

After that, Amy stopped going to most of her classes. She was going to flunk out of college anyway, she said, so why should she keep torturing herself? During the day, she and Hank drove up into the mountains and walked around the reservoir, then returned sleepy and smiling. At night, they sometimes came into the store and then we would lock the doors and sit on the counters while Hank mixed us drinks—shots with vulgar names and juicy cocktails that we slurped like soda. On nights when Hank worked late at the bar, Amy and I would smoke with the lawyers, drinking wine we bought at a store around the corner and eating Red's sister's fudge by the fistful.

The bar where Hank worked was a college bar, and I liked hearing stories about the things that happened there. The guys were always getting into fights. The girls were always crying and throwing up on themselves. Once, Hank told us, a girl and her boyfriend had gotten into a huge fight that ended with the girl climbing onto a pool table, stripping off all her clothes, and pouring a pitcher of beer over her head. "Microbrew too," Hank said. "Not cheap beer."

Hank thought that most of the kids at the college were snobby pieces of shit and told me that among the locals, drinking at the Mexican restaurant where my sister and Betty worked was known as the most expensive way to get drunk and the cheapest way to get laid.

"Hank!" Amy gasped when he said this, but I waved her quiet.

Hank told me that there were guys in this town who thought it was a pretty big thing to pick up a college girl, such a big thing, in fact, that some even kept track of how many girls they picked up so that they could compare their number with the numbers of other guys who kept track.

I imagined myself as a number on a list. Eleven. Nineteen. Twenty-eight. Just a train passing through a station—a college girl in a college bar, a girl who might go on to anywhere, to do anything.

We were sitting on the stockroom floor, and Amy looked down at the concrete. Her legs were stretched in front of her and she slid a cigarette from her pack, rolling it between her fingers as she thought.

Hank scooted one leg sideways on the floor, nudging the bottom of her foot with the bottom of his. "Not me, of course," he said, and Amy's eyes lifted. The office door was open behind her and the light hit her hair from the back, making it glow pink around her face. Her chin was cocked, her skin pale as paper, and I realized all at once that she was beautiful.

Hank lit a match for Amy's cigarette and she leaned in toward the flame. "Besides," he said as she began to inhale, "I've got the prettiest little coed on the planet. And I've got her whenever I want."

In the end, it turned out that professors at our college were not permitted to assign grades in the manner that Amy's professor had described, and he confessed, once all the paper hat businesses had closed their doors, that his whole grading technique had been, from the very beginning, nothing more than a motivational bluff. The team members of the most successful business would receive an A as promised, but the grades of the remaining four teams would be determined by a final exam.

At home, my sister and Betty uncorked a bottle of champagne and we stood in the kitchen, sipping from juice glasses. What a relief to have it all be over! And they didn't even have to take the final!

At Prairie Arts, Hank and I tried to engage Amy in a similar celebration. The news was good! She wasn't cooked!

But she was. Once she knew that her group's business was going to be in the bottom two, Amy had let everything go, even the classes she was passing. No amount of cramming could save her now. This semester would be her last.

Amy seemed strangely calm, as though she was talking about someone other than herself. Hank poured a beer into a paper cup and she held it in both hands, sipping from the foam.

It wasn't right, Amy said after a while, not right that a person could lie like that. Maybe her professor had just wanted to motivate them, she said. And maybe some people rose to the occasion or didn't take it too seriously. But there must be other people like her, she said, people whose lives got ruined because of that lie. She couldn't be the only one.

"It's not right," I agreed. "You should tell someone."

Amy's eyes shot up at the ceiling. "Sure," she snorted. "He's a professor."

"So," I said. "He's still got a boss."

Amy laughed without smiling, then shook her head no.

But Hank agreed with me. It was a fucked-up thing that guy had done and Amy had a right to say something about it.

Hank opened a bottle of wine and we sat on the floor of the stockroom, figuring out exactly how Amy should voice this injustice. I wanted to call the school newspaper, but Hank thought that Amy should go straight to the president of the college. "Just bust right in there," he said, "and tell him what you told us."

We should put it in writing, I said. That way, we could send it to as many people as we wanted, and we could take our time getting it exactly right. Amy and Hank agreed that writing a letter was the best idea, and we opened another bottle of wine and then another, working and reworking our letter until the bottles were empty and the streets were silent and we found ourselves agreeing that the best idea was not to write a letter after all, but to find Amy's professor's house and throw eggs at it.

Things went bad very quickly after that. Once we ran out of eggs, Amy began throwing rocks, and when one broke through a window, the lights snapped on inside the house. We heard a woman scream, then a child crying. I started to run but couldn't remember in which direction we had left the car, and so I stopped, squinting into the darkness for Hank and Amy.

Lights were beginning to appear in the windows of the houses next door and across the street. I heard a slight buzz and there was a sudden pop of brightness, floodlights, and Amy appeared in front of me on the lawn, ghostly white and frozen with fear. Beyond her, on the porch, the front door was open and a small, hunched man stood in white underpants, clutching a garden rake in front of himself like a weapon.

Amy's back was to me and so it was only from her professor's shifting expression that I knew their eyes had met, that the recognition had been made, and then I was yanked backward, pulled by Hank into a bar of shadow along the house across the street.

He stood behind me, one arm holding me around the waist, one hand clamped over my mouth. His chest heaved against my back and we watched Amy drop to her knees in the middle of the lawn and cover her face with her hands.

I could hear sirens in the distance, and down the block, a man began to yell. Hank took a few steps back, dragging me with him. In the darkness, he spun me around, backing me up against the wall of the house with his hand still pressed against my mouth. He looked into my eyes and, for a moment, I thought he was going to kiss me.

"Be real quiet," he whispered, and I nodded against his palm. He dropped his hand slightly, uncovering my mouth so that my chin rested on the webbing between his thumb and forefinger. His palm was pressed against my throat and I closed my eyes, waiting for the touch of his lips on mine. Then he leaned in and whispered, "Do you know where you are?"

I opened my eyes, and Hank squeezed my jaw in his hand, angling my head so that my gaze fell just over his shoulder. "You live that way," he said. "Just keep going, and you'll get home."

He stepped back and I reached for his wrist, but he shook me away, moving into the light with his hands held up above his ears. "Just being drunk and stupid, mister," he said as he walked away from me. "Just random drunk and stupid. My girl here had nothing to do with it, swear to God."

I don't know how it ended. I was gone before it ended.

Would it make a difference to say that I went back a few hours later? Not to the house—there would have been no point in that—but to the store. The sun had not yet risen, but when I arrived at Prairie Arts, the lights were on and the back door was unlocked. For a moment, my heart lightened with relief. Amy and Hank had gotten away just fine and had beaten me here to tidy up. What a riot this would be when we all saw one another! Wait until we told the lawyers!

But once I was inside the store, I knew that Amy and Hank were not there. The air was too still, the space too silent. The wine bottles and plastic cups were strewn around the stockroom floor along with empty fudge boxes and drafts of Amy's letter. Also, Red was there.

He stood very still amid the mess, an empty cigarette pack in one hand, a draft of Amy's letter in the other. I told him that I had come to clean up, and he said it was a little late for that.

I asked if Amy was okay and he told me that Amy was his business, not mine, and he would thank me very much for leaving his business to him. Then he told me that he had known girls like me his whole life—growing up in this town, of course he had. Girls like me, we all thought we were so smart, so special, and we just sat around waiting for something remarkable to happen to us. But I ought to know, he said, that no one owed me anything. I ought to know that all over this country there were towns just like this one, full of girls just like me.

He crossed to the register and I stood while he opened the drawer and removed the stack of twenties. Earlier that day, a woman from Wichita had bought a sculpture of the reservoir up in the mountains. The replica was the size of a chessboard and made of polished stone, with green, fuzzy pieces to look like trees and silvery, translucent plastic for the water. The woman who bought the sculpture asked me what I thought of it and I told her I thought it was very nice, though really I thought it was ugly and overpriced.

She told me that she had been born in this town but moved away when she was nine. As a child, her parents had taken her and her two sisters up into the mountains and they had floated on the reservoir in small rented boats and eaten sandwiches beside the water. Then she paid for the sculpture in cash and I helped her carry it to her car.

Now, Red folded the woman's money into my hand and I closed my fist around the bills, fat and heavy as a peach. When he looked at me, his eyes were tired, his face sagging. I felt, for a moment, that there was something more he wanted to say, but he shook his head and turned away.

I walked back home with the money soft and cool against my fingers, my heart fluttering each time I thought about how much was there. I didn't stop to count, but I had balanced the drawer earlier that night, and so I knew the amount. In truth, it wasn't that much money. But this all happened a while ago, before I'd begun to pay for anything, before I had any idea of what things really cost.

Sex Scenes from a Chain Bookstore

Eric Moe told me that his wife was a figure skater in her youth, and the years of punishment she'd inflicted upon her body in pursuit of landing that perfect lutz or axel or walley, the repeated slamming of bone and blade and ice, had left her with pretty serious joint deterioration that made sex a delicate operation at best. The first time I had sex with Eric Moe it was on the table in the employee lounge. As the manager, he had to stay late to count the safe and write the nightly report after the bookstore had closed. I had forgotten my wallet in my locker and had to go back inside to get it. He said it would be a onetime thing. His wife was going through an especially bad period. He hated his job. Felt disconnected from his daughter. The backs of my legs scratched on the rough edges of the table and Eric bit my lip until it bled. Afterward, he told me I was very limber.

"You're kidding?" Mara asks. She is on her knees in the

children's section, scrubbing vomit out of the carpet in yellow rubber gloves like the ones my mother used to wear to wash dishes. Mara trained me. She has been here for three years and knows the store better than anyone. Telling her about Eric isn't betrayal, it's just information.

She dips her rag into a bucket of soapy water and wrings it out over the stain on the carpet. "You know he has a kid, right?"

"April," I say. "I give her flute lessons on Thursdays."

Mara stops scrubbing and looks at me. "That's fucked-up."

I shrug. "She wants to learn how to play."

Mara lowers her voice and gives me a look. "How many times?"

"I don't know. Seven or eight."

"Where?" she whispers.

I squat down by Mara, adjusting the handle of her bucket. "The office, the stockroom, European History, Film Studies—"

"You do it here?"

"—Self-Improvement."

She clucks with her tongue.

"It's not a big deal," I tell her. "You've slept with every boy here."

She laughs. "Yeah. Both of them."

Eric Moe doesn't like to hire boys. He says they're sullen and dissatisfied, too quick to go out and find a better job.

"He won't fall in love with you," she says.

"Good," I say.

Eric Moe is too thin and too straight. Everything about him is straight. He has straight hair and straight teeth. He wears straight, thin ties and pants pressed with perfect straight creases. He uses words like *spearhead* and *eyeball* as verbs and drinks decaffeinated coffee because he says that regular makes him overly sensitive to sound. He is proud that our store is ranked first in cleanliness for our region, which I guess is good since it's ranked last in sales. After we have sex, he always tells me it's the last time.

A woman comes around the corner and holds up her hands when she sees Mara and me. "Thank God," she says. "Why are you workers so hard to find? I've been looking everywhere." She is tight, thin-lipped. All chin and nose and narrow eyes.

"Can we help you?" Mara peels off her rubber gloves.

"Yes." She hands me a book. "Is this good?"

"I haven't read it," I tell her and try to hand it back.

Mara nudges me with her elbow and smiles at the woman. "This has been a very popular title," she tells her. "Really high sales for this one. Take it home and read the first chapter. If you don't like it, you can always return it."

When the woman is gone, Mara wags her finger at me. "You don't have to be knowledgeable," she says in a singsong voice. "Just enthusiastic."

Mara knows everything about customers. When she trained me, she told me how to handle the mean ones. "Some of them just get off on being nasty. If you cry, they usually stop."

"The customer is always right?" I'd asked her.

"The customer is usually a moron," she said. "But if the boss has to choose a side, he will always choose theirs. With most of them, they just want to see that they've gotten to you. A few fake tears is all. It's not that bad."

Later, Eric's wife brings him dinner in a greasy paper bag and their daughter stands in front of me, smiling through her curtain of hair.

69

"Hi, Jillian."

"Hey, April."

April is eleven, quiet, respectful. Everything Eric's daughter should be. While Eric and the wife eat dinner in his office, she follows me through the store.

"I've been practicing," she says.

"That's great."

"I really like your shoes."

"Thanks."

"If I'd brought my flute, I could show you how much I've been practicing."

"You can show me on Thursday."

April stands on the other side of the cash register while I count the cash. She lifts herself up on the counter with her arms locked at the elbows and her feet dangling off the ground.

"I love Thursday," she says. "It's my favorite day." She clicks her toes against the side of the counter and then drops back to the floor. "Because of flute lessons."

"I'm glad," I tell her.

When she follows me back to the employee lounge, she loops her arm through mine. "You smell nice," she says and leans her head against my arm.

"It's my perfume," I tell her. We pass Mara, who is taking out the trash, and I can feel her stare on the back of my neck.

I watch the closed door of Eric's office and try to make out the sound of voices behind it. "You can try some," I tell April and gesture to my purse. "Don't go nuts, though. Your mom might not like it."

On our way out that night, I say I've forgotten my keys and go back. Mara watches me while the other girls get into their cars.

"Want me to wait?"

"Nah," I say, and she shakes her head.

Eric is sitting in front of the open safe, head down, counting the money. From where I stand I can see the freckled birthmark on the back of his neck.

"Hey."

He turns and smiles. "Well, hello there."

"I forgot my keys."

He holds one arm out to the side like I'm going to walk over to him. But I lean in the doorway and cross my arms over my chest.

"Well, you probably shouldn't walk out alone now," he says. "I'm not supposed to let you do that. For safety reasons."

I nod. "You never know what could happen out there," I say. "Rapists and murderers just waiting to attack in the bookstore parking lot."

He coughs and looks at the floor. He is not sure if I am joking. It is usually like this.

When he starts to pass me in the doorway, I rotate my ankle and follow him with my eyes. He stops and puts one hand out against the doorframe. I stare.

"Let's do it on the safe," he whispers.

"It hurts my back," I say.

He sighs and walks past me into his office. I stand and watch him straighten the papers on his desk. I point to April's school picture. "She's coming along with the flute," I say.

His arms go still and his head drops. "Don't."

I smile. "She has a very physical relationship with the music."

Eric's jaw tightens. "Stop," he says.

I take a step forward. "Probably gets it from her mom."

When he grabs my shoulders and shakes me, I say, "Let's fuck in Feminism."

On the floor, the back of my head bangs against the bookshelf and Eric laughs when I gasp. He forces his hand into my mouth and I feel the skin on my lips split as they strain and stretch. I let my teeth find the clink of his wedding band and I push at it with the flat of my tongue. Bite into the flesh around it. When he pulls his hand back, I think he is going to hit me. But instead he pulls off the ring and throws it against the shelf.

Fast. Hard. He says words I can't make out and moans when I dig my chin into the hollow of his shoulder. When we're finished, I stand in the aisle, touching my hand to my swollen mouth while Eric searches for his ring underneath the bookshelves.

"This is a mess," he says and gestures to the books that fell when I hit my head against the shelf.

"I'm off the clock."

He doesn't look at me. "Then go home. I'll fix it myself."

I'm at the computer when Angry Guy says he needs to find a book. He drums his fingers against the desk and takes short, huffy breaths. Angry Guy is an important person with important places to be. Angry Guy is in a hurry. No smiles. No chitchat. Angry Guy just wants his book. Unfortunately, Angry Guy doesn't know the title or author of the book he wants.

"It was just on TV and I think the cover is red." I look at him over the computer screen, and he snaps his fingers at me. "On TV," he says. "Not more than an hour ago. And it's red. The book is red. Did you get that, Gidget?"

Enthusiasm is not going to help me here. "Well," I say slowly. "That's lucky, because we actually organize our books by color here."

When he asks to speak to my manager, I page Eric over the intercom. He walks up smiling like a game show host, and I nod toward Angry Guy with my eyes.

Eric is all business. "I'm the manager, sir." He keeps smiling. Extends his hand. "What can I do for you?"

Angry Guy wants me fired and tells Eric so. I cross my arms. This is something that can't happen. Eric cannot fire me. The reason that Eric cannot fire me stems from the basic manager-employee code listed in our company handbook: Eric cannot fuck me.

Eric's mouth tightens and he doesn't look at me. "Jillian is one of our best employees," he tells the man. "I'm sure there has just been a misunderstanding." He steps behind the desk and Angry Guy shakes his head. It is nonnegotiable. If I keep my job, he will never shop here again.

This is the best solution I have heard so far.

Eric says that he is so sorry he had a negative experience. Just like that. "Negative experience." I feel my face begin to get hot. He says he'll have a talk with me and offers Angry Guy a gift certificate for fifty dollars. Angry Guy accepts.

Angry Guy watches me while Eric fills out the gift certificate, curling one side of his mouth into a fat little smile. This is the part that makes him very happy: my boss apologizing to him for my bad behavior, making it up to him, letting him watch while I wait for my spanking.

"That girl nearly cost you a customer," he says to Eric. "I hope you give her something to think about."

As Eric hands the man his certificate, he puts his foot

over mine under the counter and lightly presses it down onto my toes.

When we're alone, he touches my elbow and winks at me. "Don't be a bitch to our customers."

That night we do it in Crafts and Hobbies and when Eric rips my blouse I tell him that his wife is going to leave him. It's a woman thing, I say. I can just tell.

"You're pissed about that customer earlier," he says.

"She makes more money than you do. Maybe she'll give you alimony."

"I have a boss too, you know. I tell some customer to fuck off and he would just go above my head."

"Think how much easier it will be," I say as he digs his fingers into my hair and pulls it hard in fistfuls, "when you only have to father on weekends and occasional holidays."

He pushes me backward with so much force that the shelf shakes and flower art books waterfall down on us as he pins me to the floor.

"He wanted me to fire you," he hisses.

"So fire me."

Afterward, we stand in front of my car while Eric writes me a check for April's flute lessons. He tears the check off and blows at the ink. "You're a snake," he says. "Drive carefully."

Mara is using the phone in the stockroom to prank-call the store. She holds her finger over her lips to silence me and when she speaks her voice is thick and affected.

"Yes," she says into the phone. "I'm looking for a book." She says the author's name and the title and then gives me the thumbs-up sign. "I'm on hold," she tells me.

The thick voice comes back when she starts to talk again.

"I'm not positive that's the one, hon," she says. "Could you just read me the back of it?"

Of course, Mara is positive that's the one since we spent the last fifteen minutes searching through Romance to find the book with the most graphic description printed on the back.

Mara covers the receiver with her hand and holds the phone to the side so that we can both listen to Jake, who is a new hire.

". . . But Randolph throbs with longing to make the chaste Muriel his own. Only his desire is stronger than her will. And in the thrust of one heaving summer, they defy her uncle and join their passion in the vineyards of her inheritance."

After she hangs up with Jake, Mara tells me that I ought to go look like I'm working. "If you slack too much and Eric doesn't say anything, people will put it together."

I dust in Classics until it is my turn to get the phones. The first caller is a man who needs a book on restoring 1970s Fiats. He says he saw it in the store three weeks ago.

"Someone might have bought it between then and now," I tell him.

"No one bought it," he says.

"I'll have to go look." I don't want to go look.

"I'll wait," he says.

I have to get on my knees to search the shelves, and I bump against men's legs as I run my finger along the spines of books. Two different men step on my hand while I am on the floor.

"Do you have to do this right now?" one asks.

It takes almost fifteen minutes, but I finally find it. It's skinny and bent at the corners, crammed between two motorcycle books.

"I have it in my hand," I tell the man when I pick up the phone.

"It took you long enough," he says.

"I'll hold it for you." I am searching through the drawers to find pen and paper so that I can write his name down.

"Don't bother," he says. "I'll come in later tonight."

I am not going to look for the book again. I found it once. I shouldn't have to find it again in an hour. "I can't guarantee that it will be here if I don't hold it for you," I tell him.

"Why's that?" His voice is dull, humorless.

"Someone might buy it."

"Listen, Gidget, no one will buy it."

Aha. Angry Guy. After he hangs up, I take the book and reshelve it in the Cooking section.

"This night sucks," I tell Jake when I get back to the desk.

"Yeah," he says. "Some gross bitch made me read a romance novel to her over the phone."

When I hear him, he's already yelling. "I talked to some girl! She found it less than an hour ago!"

"I'm sorry, sir. I can't find it," Mara says. Her voice is small in comparison to his, breathy and light. "Maybe someone bought it between then and now."

Angry Guy pounds his fist on the desk. "It's the most obscure book in history," he shouts. "Nobody fucking bought it! Look again."

As I walk up to them, I can see Mara's chin beginning to pucker, her eyes reddening around the rims.

"What's the problem here?" I ask.

"You," he says. "I talked to you." Customers around us

have gone strangely still, staring over the tops of their open books. "You told me on the phone that you had a book."

"We're very busy here, sir," I say evenly. "I've talked to a lot of people on the phone."

"You remember, sweetheart." His voice is thick and wet and he touches his tongue to the corner of his mouth. "I'm sure you do."

"I remember."

"Well, she can't find it." He points at Mara and instantly her lip begins to tremble.

I look back at the man and shrug. "Someone must have purchased it."

His face hardens and his frame squares. "No one purchased it," he says.

Customers are beginning to exchange looks with one another. They think he's a lunatic. Some nutball who makes scenes in public places. His pupils narrow and I stare at him. "We could order it for you," I say. "It would be here in five to seven business days."

He takes a step toward me and I can feel his breath on my face. "It's here," he hisses. "I saw it here three weeks ago."

I keep smiling. "Maybe you should have purchased it then."

Eric is moving toward us like he's on wheels, his eyes darting between us and the customers watching. "What's the problem?" he asks Mara, who has dropped back behind me.

I feel Eric at my elbow, trying to move between us, but I take a step closer, sugar my voice, show him my teeth, and stare hard.

"You gonna do something about this?" he asks Eric, but I take another step closer.

"Now, sir," I begin, slowly, like to a child. "I'm trying to help you." I talk louder, loud enough that everyone listening can hear. "But this is a public place and I am going to need you to lower your voice and be a gentleman."

His lips are hard white lines when he grabs my neck. I hear people gasp. My eyes and tongue push forward and my eyelids go taut. My heartbeat is in my temples, my lips, the bridge of my nose, and the light dims around his face. It isn't until my head hits the ground that I hear the sound of Eric's fist, the wet noise it makes as it hits again and again, and I feel Mara's hands on my face.

Eric and I stay late to fill out the nightly report. He is sitting at the desk and I sit on the floor with my back against the office door. My neck feels ropy and long and my head rocks on top of it. The report is blank on the desk and Eric is smoking.

"I'll lose my job," he says. His eyes are swollen; he watches an empty space on the wall.

"You hate your job," I tell him, and he ashes into a foam cup.

"I hit him. I could get sued. The whole company could get sued."

My tongue is thick and dry and I can feel my heartbeat in the back of my throat. I try to steady my head with my forearms.

Eric stubs his cigarette out on a pad of Post-its, then blows the ash onto the carpeting. "My wife is going to leave me."

I stare up at the fluorescent lights, the water-stained ceiling. I can't think of a single thing to say.

He blinks at me and taps his pen on the empty report. I extend my leg in front of me, but my foot doesn't quite reach his and he looks down at the place where we almost touch. Tomorrow is Thursday and in the afternoon I will listen to April play scales on her flute. I will wear a turtleneck so that she won't see the marks under my chin, the bruises on my neck. I will let her watch MTV. I will let her try on my clothes. We will make cookies and root beer floats.

But now, right now, we sit like this, Eric and I, almost touching, not saying anything.

Captain's Club

To be clear: Tommy Whittaker was not best friends with CJ Franklin, not any kind of friends, really. So when CJ announced that he could bring another boy along on the Mediterranean cruise he was taking with his father and his father's girlfriend over spring break, the notion that this other boy might end up being Tommy was absurd. Absolutely absurd. CJ Franklin was a ballplayer—foot, basket, base—and his top choices were too: Will Barber, then Brian Hess, Zane Dixon, and Kyle Raber. Next came the Wilson twins (first Dax, then Bo), then Chris Whiteside, Lucas Cordova, and Josh Sigler. Tommy had known them all since kindergarten, had ridden the school bus with them and belonged to the same Cub Scout troop, back in the scouting days. But that was forever ago, elementary school, a different life.

This was middle school, seventh grade, and CJ and his friends had grown taller, lanky and long-limbed with large, flapping feet and faces splattered with pimples. Tommy was still just Tommy, a small boy with dimpled knees and hair so fine it looked like feathers. In the locker room after gym class, CJ and his friends waited turns for the showers and Tommy could see the shadows of hair beginning on their chests and underarms, could smell the sweat, like onion soup, rising off their naked backs. Tommy would sniff at his own armpit, pink and hairless as a pencil eraser, then creep past the showers to change clothes in the privacy of a toilet stall.

All of CJ's friends wanted to go with CJ to the Mediterranean for spring break. But their mothers had concerns about the boys traveling so far—out of the country!—without them; about CJ's father, who lived in Chicago and rarely visited; about this "girlfriend," who was not, apparently, the same girlfriend who last year accompanied CJ and his father to San Diego.

No one had any interest in expressing these concerns directly to CJ's mother, who was reactive and unreasonable and had a habit of taking things personally. So came the excuses: Will Barber already had plans for a camping trip over spring break with an older cousin from California; Brian Hess was entered in a karate tournament; Zane Dixon had a bike race; the twins—first Dax, then Bo—were scheduled to have their wisdom teeth removed; and Chris Whiteside and Lucas Cordova were both going to visit their grandmothers. Josh Sigler, his mother said, got nosebleeds on boats.

For her part, CJ's mother—once she had gotten over her initial fury at her ex-husband's extravagance in (1) booking this ridiculous cruise in the first place, and (2) allowing their son to bring a friend along—was determined to see a friend go. As long as another boy went along, CJ could enjoy himself with someone who was not his father or his father's girlfriend.

All in all, sixteen mothers said no before Tommy's mother— maybe because, unlike the other mothers, she had not been

expecting the call and therefore had no time to really consider the details from every angle before responding, or maybe
because she didn't exactly have her senses together to consider such details anyway, maybe because this was the year
Tommy's father had left and she was lonely and tired and raw-
faced from crying, because there wasn't enough money and
the porch was rotting and Tommy's little sisters both needed
braces, because it might be good for Tommy to spend some
time with another boy, with another boy's father, because
Tommy was sweet and good and deserved a little sunshine
after this gray, miserable winter, because the trip was to the
Mediterranean (and when would she ever be able to take him
to the Mediterranean?)—said yes. Yes, Tommy could go.

Cash was short, but Tommy's mother wanted him to have the
right things for the cruise, so she bought him three new pairs
of shorts and a tube of good sunblock and a little camera of
his very own. She packed eight rolls of film into his suitcase
and told him to take lots of pictures.

At the airport, Tommy's mother kneeled to hug him good-
bye while his little sisters stood on either side of her, sucking on their fingers. Tommy's mother took his hands in hers,
kissing the inside of each of his palms. She was not at all
beautiful, Tommy's mother, but she was kind and gentle and
fragile as a bird. Tommy would be gone for two weeks—
never had he been apart from her for so long. Her kisses
were warm and damp in the palms of his hands, and he felt
a fire of panic sweep through himself as he realized that he
was about to cry.

He had worried about this, that he would not be able to
part from her without tears, but somewhere in the back of

his mind he had harbored a secret hope that CJ might be similarly distraught when faced with leaving his own mother. Tommy had thought that he and CJ might comfort each other, that they might make it through together.

Now, though, it was clear that this was not to be the case.

CJ played his Game Boy with his shoulders hunched while his mother fussed around him, checking the ID tags on his luggage and the zippers on his backpack. CJ's mother was tall and broad-shouldered, with large, white teeth and lips as red as raw steak. She told CJ to be cautious and safe and to ask himself before making any decision whether it was the decision that she, his mother, would make for him. CJ's father, she reminded CJ, was not exactly Mr. Reliable. And he was selfish and vindictive besides.

Their flight began to board, and Tommy's mother folded a twenty-dollar bill into his hand and whispered that he should find something small to bring back for his sisters. A wave of anguish washed through him as he realized that he had not brought money to buy a gift for his mother. As if reading his thoughts, she put her hands on either side of his face, smoothing his hair off his forehead. "Remember everything," she told him, "and bring it all home to me."

Next to them, CJ's mother pulled CJ against her, smashing his face between her massive breasts. She held him there, arms locked around his neck, chin hooked over the top of his head. "Remember where you belong," she said finally. "And if that shithead says one word against me, you kick him right in the nuts."

In the end, Tommy didn't cry. But he wanted to and that was bad enough.

Usually, Tommy was the color of milk, with skin so pale that his veins showed blue along his jaw and beneath his eyes. But when he was upset, his skin turned red in patches that burned like a rash. As he followed CJ down the Jetway, Tommy could feel the heat spreading across his chest and arms, creeping up his neck. By the time they'd reached their seats, Tommy's whole face was engulfed in flames of anguish, his throat filling with a river of lava. His nose began to run, and he wiped it on his shoulder and turned his face away from CJ, his hands cold and quivering in his lap.

The time passed and Tommy felt the sorrow begin to settle inside him like silt. CJ had brought a Game Boy and a Discman and enough batteries, games, and CDs to keep him occupied for the whole plane ride. Tommy had brought a notebook and a pen to help him remember everything that happened. Now he opened the notebook and angled his body sideways so that CJ would not be able to see. Tommy wrote the date and the time and then, *Sitting on the airplane, drinking a 7UP. They're going to feed us lunch soon.*

The air inside the plane was cool and dry, and Tommy's mind began to drift in and out of a half-sleep from which he would awaken suddenly, disoriented and thinking about his mother. He pictured her at home, heating up dinner or washing the dishes. Since his father had left, there was a silence inside their house, a quiet he could feel on his skin like a damp, chilly fog.

Still, there were moments when Tommy's mother would lift out of it all, moments when the clouds cleared behind her eyes and she would call him to her. Then she would push his hair off his forehead with her fingers and tell him that he was her champion, her white knight, her hero, and Tommy would flex his skinny arms while she clapped and cheered and whistled.

The thought of this now, on the airplane, stirred the sorrow inside Tommy and he felt it begin to brew and bubble in his stomach, moving through his throat, into his sinuses, and up through the corners of his eyes. He leaned forward onto his tray table and buried his face in his arms, hoping that CJ would think he was trying to sleep.

In Rome, CJ's father was waiting for them at Customs. He leaned against the wall, tall and narrow-chested, with thick, dark hair like CJ's and short, square feet that splayed out like a duck's. When he saw them, he stretched his arms wide on either side of himself and rocked back on his heels. "Dudes!"

Tommy stood to the side while CJ and his father slapped five and punched each other on the shoulders. CJ's father asked if they were ready to have some fun, and CJ mumbled something Tommy couldn't understand.

"Tree's outside," said CJ's father, "waiting in the car."

"Who?" asked CJ.

"My friend. Tree."

"Her name is *Tree*?"

"Yeah, Tree," CJ's father said, then looked at his wrist as if to check the time, though he wasn't wearing a watch. "You know, like tree."

CJ blinked at his father, who then turned to Tommy, shaking his hand so hard that Tommy's arm wobbled up in his shoulder joint. "Cal Franklin," he said. "But my pals call me Frank, and you can call me that too."

Tommy's suitcase was an old one of his mother's with a broken handle and two broken wheels, so that he had to part scoot, part carry it through the airport. By the time they reached the car, his arms were burning and his hair was damp with sweat. CJ's father loaded their bags into the trunk, then turned and took CJ by the shoulders. "Let me really get a look at you," he said. Then he started to cry.

Tommy crawled into the backseat of the car, shutting the door behind him as quietly as he could. Inside, the motor was running and the air conditioner washed over him like a cool bath. He heard a rustle of fabric, and then a scent, sweet and pretty like a garden, swept across his face as a woman turned from the front seat to smile at him. "Are you CJ?"

"I'm Tommy," he said and pointed out the window to where CJ stood, his spine rigid, in his father's embrace. "That's CJ."

Tree turned to look. "Wow," she said after a moment. "He's really big."

Tommy nodded. "He's good at sports."

"Maybe I should climb back there with you," Tree said, squinting into the backseat. "There's more leg room up here." She bit the inside of her lip, cupping her chin in one hand. "That's what I should do, right?"

Before Tommy could answer, she hiked one skinny leg and then the other between the two front seats and hoisted herself through. Her skirt slid up around her thighs, and Tommy stared down at her knees, white and creamy as two pieces of fruit.

"I've never been on a cruise," she said.

"Me neither," Tommy told her. She smiled at him and he felt a sudden lightening inside himself, a bit of stale air releasing from someplace deep within.

"I bought all new outfits," Tree said, bunching the fabric of her skirt in her hands.

"These shorts are new," Tommy told her, and she leaned

back to look. The shorts were green-and-yellow plaid and had come from Kmart. He had an identical pair in blue-and-red plaid and another in solid blue.

"I like them a lot," she said at last. "They make you look carefree."

CJ's father and Tree had spent the day in Rome and had seen the Sistine Chapel and the Pietà, which, CJ's father was sorry to report, was just a statue. But, he said, winking at Tree in the rearview mirror, they had managed to pass through the Vatican without getting struck by lightning.

Tree glanced nervously in the direction of CJ, who had yet to acknowledge her. "Worse people than us have been through the Vatican," she said.

CJ's father laughed. "Baby, worse people than us are buried at the Vatican."

On board, their cabin was small and crowded with a bed for Tree and CJ's father and a convertible sofa that, when made up for CJ and Tommy to share, removed every single inch of floor space from the room.

"We won't have to spend much time here," Tree assured them as she leafed through folders and flyers about the ship and all its services. A morning newsletter would tell them what activities were available both on board and at their daily port of call. There were lectures and tours and exhibits, hikes to the rims of volcanoes and dives through underwater caves. In the evenings, the ship would set sail for their next port, and they would have dinner on board and see a live show. The only time they would all be in this room, Tree said, was when they were sleeping. And then they wouldn't care how cramped they were. Right?

CJ looked sideways at Tommy, horrified. "We have to share a bed?"

Tommy felt suddenly sick with loneliness—he wanted his mother, his bedroom, his place at the dinner table. The ship had not set sail yet, and he wondered what it might take to get him on the next plane home. "I've changed my mind," he could tell them, or, "I forgot my insulin." Tommy was not diabetic, but no one had to know that.

Before he could speak, Tree gasped, clutching her hands together beneath her chin. At the end of the cruise, she read aloud, there was a formal night. Women had to wear gowns and men tuxedos. She looked up at CJ's father. "Oh Frank, promise we'll all go!"

The ship's motors grumbled to life somewhere deep beneath them, and Tommy could feel the sudden hum up through the soles of his feet. "I don't have a tuxedo," he said.

Tree clapped her hands as she read from the folder. "We can rent them on the ship!—gowns too!—oh Frank!" She turned, lifting up onto her toes to look at him. "Promise right now that we will!"

CJ's father gave her a thin smile and patted the small of her back. "I don't know if these dudes want to get dressed up in monkey suits," he said, raising one eyebrow at CJ. Tommy could tell that CJ's father had hoped to win a little of CJ's approval by objecting to tuxedos, and CJ must have sensed this too, for he looked down at his feet and refused to comment.

When it became clear that CJ was not going to express an opinion about the formal night, his father looked to Tommy. Behind CJ's father, Tree pressed her palms together in a silent plea, then giggled, covering her lips with her hand.

"I think it sounds fun," Tommy said, and CJ's shoulders stooped.

"Tuxedos are gay," he mumbled.

"James *Bond* wears a tuxedo," Tree told him.

"My dad likes James Bond," Tommy said, but as soon as he spoke he remembered it was James Dean and not James Bond whom his father liked. CJ looked at Tommy and his eyes narrowed.

Tommy imagined CJ's great, raw-boned fist bludgeoning his face and he started to take back his endorsement of the formal night. But CJ's father was already brushing his lips against Tree's hairline, conceding. And then Tree leaned around him and gave Tommy a small, secret smile, sealing the deal completely.

Their first dinner on the ship passed one creeping moment at a time. Tree and Tommy ate in silence while CJ's father told stories about himself and asked CJ questions that CJ mostly didn't answer:

"How's school?"

"Okay."

"Teachers pretty good?"

"I guess."

"Who's your favorite team this season?"

"I don't know."

Then CJ's father began to go on about baseball and the amazing seats he got free through his job. CJ should come to Chicago this summer, his father said, and they could catch some games. The seats were top-notch.

After dinner, they all walked to the theater to see the show, but when they reached the entrance, CJ's father stretched his hands above his head and said that live theater wasn't really his thing. He thought he might check out the casino and catch up with them later.

Tree turned after him, her forehead creased, her lips parted. But before she could object, CJ started in the opposite direction, mumbling something about the arcade. Tree stood, looking back and forth between them, then turned to Tommy, helpless. "Is it okay if he goes off by himself?" she asked, pointing after CJ.

Tommy shrugged. It was okay with him.

Inside the theater they ordered lemonades and sat together at a little table. The show was bright and shiny, full of dancers and acrobats and songs that everyone in the audience knew and sang along to. Afterward, the muscles in Tommy's face hurt from smiling, and the palms of his hands stung as he clapped harder and harder. Everywhere he looked, people were happy and laughing. Children bounced on their parents' shoulders and couples walked arm in arm, sweet and snuggling. Tree hummed one of the songs from the show, swinging her purse lightly from her wrist. "I'm not really ready to go to bed yet," she said.

"Me neither," Tommy told her.

"Maybe we should have another lemonade and go look at the stars."

Up on the deck, the sky was black as felt and the air was soft and damp on Tommy's skin. They walked along the rows of empty deck chairs, sipping from their straws. When they reached the back of the ship, they stopped, resting their elbows on the railing to look out at the vast darkness behind them. Tree leaned forward slightly, looking down at the water below.

Tommy followed her gaze down and felt a blade of fear

slash through him. The water was far below, white and churning and loud as a machine. "I wonder what would happen if you went overboard," Tree said.

Tommy imagined himself falling, his body slapping into the water.

"Can you swim?" Tree asked, and Tommy told her that he could—he used to take lessons at the YMCA. "You'd last longer than I would," she said, "long enough to watch the ship disappear, maybe."

He could picture it, the ship, bright as a city, moving deeper and deeper into the darkness, leaving him behind.

The wind blew Tree's hair across her face as she looked down into the water. "You'd know that no one was coming for you. You'd know there was no hope. What would you even think about?"

"My mom," said Tommy, and all at once he ached for her.

Tree turned, her face falling slack when she saw the sudden reddening on his throat and cheeks, the tremble in his bottom lip. "Oh no," she said. "Oh, Tommy. I'm sorry. I didn't mean to scare you."

He wiped his eyes with the backs of his hands—he wasn't scared. "I miss my mom is all," he told her.

Tree wrapped her arms around him and he could feel the rails of her hip bones through the fabric of her skirt. "Of course you miss your mom," she said. "You'll have to find something really nice to bring back to her as a present."

"I have to get something for my sisters too," he said, sliding the twenty-dollar bill from his pocket to show her. "I only have this much."

"We'll find the perfect thing for each of them," she promised. "Shopping for strangers happens to be a special talent of mine."

Tommy smiled. Tree had said *we*. They would do it together.

Tree leaned on the railing, looking back out over the water. "Frank and CJ will want to spend a lot of time together on this trip," she said.

"I know," said Tommy, though he had seen little evidence of this so far.

"They have so much catching up to do."

"Sure," he said.

Tree cocked her head at him. "I think that you and I should decide right now that we're just going to see everything there is to see and try everything there is to try and give them plenty of space to reconnect."

"Okay," Tommy told her.

She held out one hand and he shook it. "Okay," she said.

Tommy began to feel light and sleepy, as though a great weight were lifting off him. Beside him, Tree stretched her arms out, extending her fingers and tilting her chin up at the starless sky. "Isn't this the most amazing air you've ever felt in your life?" she asked. "You can't tell where your skin stops and the rest of the world begins."

Every day, their ship docked in a different port and they ate breakfast on board while Tree read through the daily newsletter, listing their options and lamenting the fact that they could not do everything. There were snorkeling excursions and hikes to ancient altars, walking tours to museums and buses to points of interest. "To come all this way," Tree said each morning as she weighed the choices, "and only have one day!"

Onshore, they wandered through ruins and were led on

guided tours of churches and palaces and mosques. Tommy kept the little camera always with him, and he snapped photos of the food they ate and the guides who led them and the view of their ship from the bus windows. Every so often, Tree would take the camera from Tommy and pose him in front of a marble sculpture or a stone fountain or a tree with pink flowers on it. *"Smile,"* she begged, but it didn't seem right.

Tommy couldn't help but imagine his mother looking through these pictures later, her thin fingers and sad eyes moving across the prints while his sisters hovered on either side, sucking their thumbs or the ends of their hair. How would it look to them, him grinning away in shorts and shirtsleeves? Tommy at the Parthenon! Tommy on a donkey! Tommy buying corn on the cob from a street vendor!

Tree pointed the camera and Tommy stood with his shoulders square and his posture straight, then fixed his mind on serious things—eggplant and doctors' offices, newspapers and the color brown.

"You look like an old man," she told him as she handed the camera back. "Seriously, my grandpa makes that face."

In the afternoons, CJ and his father would grow bored with sightseeing and head back to the ship while Tommy stayed ashore with Tree, wandering around the sun-soaked islands, eating in little restaurants, and browsing through shops. While they were on their own, Tree tried to help Tommy find gifts for his mother and his sisters. She asked questions about them, and Tommy did his best to answer.

How old were his sisters?

Lu was nine and Jeannie would turn seven this summer.

Did they have long hair or short?

Long.

Were they good at school?

Tommy wasn't sure but thought probably, since he could not remember either of them complaining much about it.

Did they take lessons?

Until this year, Lu took piano and Jeannie was in ballet. But now they were short on money and they'd all had to quit their lessons.

No more swim class at the YMCA had been fine with Tommy. His lessons met at the same time as the Silver Slippers Water Aerobics class and the sight of all those veiny legs and sagging stomachs, those arms draped with crepey sheets of flesh, made him feel light-headed and loose in his joints. The cement floors in the locker room were wet and cold and crumbly with age, and the whole place stank of mildew. Once, after class, Tommy had watched a man with a stooped back peel off his swim trunks and pick at crusty stitches on the head of his penis, and then Tommy had puked into his towel.

Now, for the first time, he wondered if his sisters might have liked their lessons, if they might miss them. Wasn't there a ballerina on Jeannie's lunch box? Not a child's ballerina, pink and pretty like a cupcake, but a real picture of a real woman, arms lifted, legs extended, body hard and lean and tough as a piece of lead pipe. The idea that his sisters might have their own thoughts and wants and disappointments had never occurred to Tommy, and he found it depressing—something else he couldn't shoulder, something else he couldn't fix.

But as promised, Tree found the perfect gifts: a porcelain hair barrette in the shape of a dolphin for Lu, and a wooden marionette for Jeannie, so light and delicate in its joints that it seemed to really leap and twirl from its strings.

Tree told Tommy that she used to work at a clothing store

in Chicago, and a big part of her job was helping men pick gifts for their wives and girlfriends. "They wouldn't have the first clue where to begin," she said. "Wouldn't know their wife's style or her favorite color or even her dress size. I would have to ask, is your wife larger than I am or smaller? Taller or shorter? What color is her hair? What's her favorite restaurant? Her favorite drink?

"I've had lots of jobs," Tree said, "but I was really good at that one. Men would come back in to tell me how happy their wives or girlfriends were, how many points they'd won for picking out the right gift for once. That's how I met Frank."

"Who was he shopping for?" Tommy asked, and Tree's eyes darted sideways at him.

"Oh," she said and waved her hand. "I forget. His sister or something. I remember the gift, though—red suede jacket, size four, expensive."

In regular life, Tommy knew that he was strange-looking, and he often feared that he was altogether ugly. At school, the other boys glowered behind mops of dark, sweaty curls, but Tommy's hair was thin and white, his brows and lashes nearly translucent against his pale skin, giving his face the smooth, expressionless quality of an egg.

"You and I will have to be extra careful about the sun," Tree had told him on their first day. "We're almost albinos—we'll burn to crisps."

Outside, she wore a shawl over her shoulders and a chocolate-colored sunhat with a wide brim that Tommy thought made her look like a movie star. Tommy wore the sunscreen his mother had bought for him, and by the end of the first week, his skin had darkened to a deep gold. His hair, once limp and colorless, now looked light and silvery against his tan. "You get any darker," CJ's father joked, "and you'll look like a photographic negative."

At home, Tommy tried to avoid looking too long at himself in the mirror, for his reflection stirred in him a feeling of great loneliness and a fear that this loneliness might be permanent. Now, though, Tommy paused to glance at himself in every reflective surface he passed. There he was, the new Tommy, tan and handsome, surrounded by beautiful people.

Their first night on the ship, Tommy had been afraid that he would not be able to fall asleep, that if he did, he would roll into CJ or brush against CJ, and then CJ would beat him to a bloody pulp. But the motion of the ship soothed Tommy's mind and relaxed his body. Almost as soon as his head met the pillow, he melted into a sweet, dreamless sleep from which he awakened every day feeling longer and looser in his body, warm and content and ready for whatever lay ahead.

"I'm not making this up," Tree told him. "You've grown an inch since I met you."

After dinner each night, CJ's father would head to the casino and CJ to the arcade, and Tree and Tommy would make their way to the theater, where they sat together, sipping lemonade while they watched the jugglers and comics and magicians. Tommy would feel Tree beside him, soft and sweet and smelling like a garden, and the happiness rolled out of him in waves.

On days when their ship stayed at sea, Tree and Tommy swam in the pool and took classes on sushi making and fruit carving and wine tasting. ("Sorry, Tommy!" Tree whispered after the class began. "I didn't know *tasting* meant 'wine tasting.'") But Tommy didn't mind. He nibbled at little pieces of cheese and fish and chocolate, and helped

Tree by sniffing her wineglass and telling her which food to choose. Soon everyone in the class was watching while he closed his eyes and breathed into Tree's glass, holding the scent on the back of his tongue until the right answer floated up behind his eyes—olive, pear, walnut—and then everyone applauded.

"I wish you could have seen it," Tree told CJ's father back in the cabin. "Tommy's a wine prodigy or something. Kemal was so impressed."

"Who's Kemal?" asked CJ's father, and Tree told him that Kemal was their tasting teacher, a waiter on the ship, and a certified expert.

The next day, they were caught in a rainstorm on an island where the city looked like white snow atop high, high cliffs. Tree and Tommy had wandered away from their tour into a quiet part of the town with small gardens and chapels and laundry hanging on clotheslines. They saw the rain moving across the water toward them in deep, purple fingers, smelled the damp, ripe release of it, and ran through the sandy little streets, their feet slapping the stone sidewalks as they searched for a place to take shelter.

There was a rumble, then a flash of lightning, and one raindrop hit Tommy's arm, warm and fat as a cup of bath-water. A few feet ahead of him, Tree squealed and pulled Tommy beneath a stone porch just as the sky darkened and the water poured down in deafening sheets. Tommy stood, pressed against Tree beneath that tiny covering, their chests heaving, their bodies damp with rain and sweat. They watched the rain fall on the white buildings and the violet ocean, the gardens and patios and flower-lined verandas, and Tommy felt that everything, the whole world and every-one in it, had been created just for him, so that he could have this moment, and he and Tree could live through it together.

On their second-to-last day, Tree and Tommy returned to the ship, leaving CJ and his father at a McDonald's onshore. The sky was cloudy, the wind picking up for another possible storm, and Tree took off her brown sunhat, holding it limply by the brim. "Tomorrow's our last day," she said finally, and Tommy fought the tightness beginning in his chest. He could not think of saying good-bye to her.

"We still haven't found anything for my mom," he said, and Tree told him they had time.

She'd been asking Tommy questions about his mother (What did her bedroom look like? Where did she grow up? Who would play her in a movie?) and he had tried to answer (messy; Kansas; the mom from *Who's the Boss?* if the actress were shorter and skinnier). But so far, this had led to nothing. "Your mother," Tree said, "is a tough nut."

Back on board, a sign outside the Main Hall announced that the Captain's Tea was being held inside. "What's that?" asked Tommy, and Tree said she didn't know—there had been nothing in the newsletter.

"Maybe it's only for captains," she said. But when they looked, the Fergusons from their sushi class were sitting at one of the tables. Before Tommy could think of an explanation, one of the waiters turned and waved them inside. "It's Kemal!" Tree said and waved back to him.

Kemal kissed Tree on the hand and bowed to Tommy. They would have the best table, he said as he sat them next to the window, because Tommy was his star pupil.

Another waiter brought a tray of small, crustless sandwiches and a pot of tea, and they sat, stirring lumps of sugar into their cups and nibbling at their sandwiches. "I'm not ready to go home yet," Tree said.

"Me neither," Tommy told her.

Tree's teacup trembled in her fingers and she put it back down on the saucer, then lifted her napkin and pressed it into her eyes. "Are you crying?" Tommy asked.

"I'm sorry," she said.

"I don't mind."

Tree took a slow breath, her chin puckered, her lips wobbling as she tried to calm herself. Tommy sipped from his cup, waiting for her to speak and wondering what he should say if she didn't.

"I quit my job to come on this trip," she said finally. "Another job. I just quit it. To come on a cruise." She pressed the pads of her fingers over her lips. "I can't stop," she said. "I can't stop ruining my life."

Her face sagged with misery, her eyes looked lost and lonely, and Tommy searched himself for the answer, the words that would help her or mend her or give her hope. It fell to him to do this, to save her, to give her his whole, entire truth.

"I love you," he said.

Her eyes moved to his, straight into his, and for a moment he felt that this was going to be one of those miraculous, significant milestones, more so even than the time he saw his fifth-grade teacher's nipple through her dress. But then Kemal was standing beside their table, telling them not to forget the Captain's Club Reception the following night in the art gallery right before the formal dinner.

Tree blinked for a moment at Tommy, then turned to Kemal, blushing as she explained that they weren't members of the Captain's Club, that they had crashed the Captain's Tea. But Kemal said it didn't matter. He would be at the door and he would let them in. They had to come, he said. There would be champagne and dancing.

"That reception isn't a big deal," CJ's father told Tree when they all met back in the cabin before dinner. "It's just a cheesy party for people who go on a lot of cruises."

Tree pressed her lips together in determination. "I don't care," she said. "It's *invitation only,* and Tommy and I got invited. If you two play your cards right, we might just bring you along as our dates."

CJ looked up from his game. "I'm not going anywhere as your date," he told Tommy.

"How did you get invited?" CJ's father asked, and Tree smiled up at him through her eyelashes.

"Maybe I've been making friends."

Their dinner should have been an ordinary dinner followed by an ordinary night, and it would have been, except that during the soup course, Kemal came to their table and told Tree that she was the most beautiful woman on the ship. Then he gave her a bracelet made of bright blue stones with black centers. Kemal fastened the bracelet around Tree's tiny wrist and stood holding her hand between his.

"You're giving this to me?" Tree asked.

Tommy's grip tightened on his soup spoon as Kemal traced his finger along the stones. They were nazars, he said, and would protect her from the evil eye.

Underneath the table, CJ's father nudged Tommy with his knee. "Who's that joker?" he asked.

After dinner, CJ headed to the arcade as usual, but his father skipped the casino and came instead to the show. Inside the theater, CJ's father sat with his arm around Tree's shoulder and Tommy had to scoot to the side to make room. Instead of lemonade, Tree drank champagne, first one glass, then another, then another. During the final number, Tommy watched CJ's father move his hand from Tree's shoulder to the flat space between her shoulder blades, stroking the back of her neck with one knuckle.

After the show, Tommy followed behind while Tree and CJ's father stumbled down the hallway to their cabin. When they reached the door, Tree went inside and CJ's father turned, blocking Tommy in the hallway. "Hey, dude," he said. "How about doing me a little favor?" He pulled a fifty-dollar bill from his pocket and crumpled it into Tommy's hand. "Go have some fun in the arcade and let me have a little time with my lady."

Everything inside Tommy felt like it was siphoning through some great drain beneath his feet. He closed his fist around the money and CJ's father disappeared inside the cabin, shutting the door behind him.

A moment later, the door opened and Tree slipped into the hallway, her feet bare, her hair mussed around her face. Tommy dropped his fist behind his back, hiding the money.

"Tommy!" she whispered, and he could smell her, the fruit and flowers, the musk of her sweat. She leaned forward, reaching for his empty hand. Her skin was warm and moist against his, and she stretched one leg behind herself, holding the door open with her bare foot. "Here," she breathed and dropped the bracelet into his palm. "Give this to your mother."

Then she went back inside, leaving Tommy alone in the hallway.

And maybe he thought that night while he was walking the deck alone about throwing them both overboard, the bracelet and the fifty-dollar bill, about winding his arm and hurling them over the rail, the money fluttering into the darkness, the bracelet sinking to the bottom of the ocean, lost forever as so many things must have been lost before.

But he didn't do it. The bracelet was delicate and beautiful, and Tommy knew that his mother would cherish it. And fifty dollars, even if it came from the person Tommy most hated in all the world, was still fifty dollars.

The next morning, Tommy vowed that he would not look at Tree or speak to her. This was the final day of their trip and everyone seemed out of sorts. CJ's father slumped over his coffee, massaging his temples with his thumbs. Tree's eyes were red, her voice husky as she read through the daily newsletter.

The formal dinner was tonight, Tree said, and CJ's father groaned—did they have to go?

Of course they had to go, Tree said. They'd ordered tuxedos.

CJ's father wanted to spend the day on the main island, but Tree hoped to take a ferry to the smaller island where they could see relics from an ancient civilization.

"Whoopee," said CJ's father. "More ruins."

When they got off the ship, the wind was blowing and the sky was the color of chalk. Tree's skirt whipped up around her hips and she grasped at it with her hands, flattening her purse against herself to hold it down.

Their tour guide for the day was Amaryllis, who was tall with green eyes and dark hair that fell straight down her back in a thick, shiny braid. She was dressed in khaki shorts that showed her legs, firm and tan, and hiking boots with solid soles. Amaryllis explained that the ferry ride to the small island was choppy and they would most likely get wet. CJ's father nudged CJ with his shoulder and whispered, "Now you can tell your friends you've seen a real Greek goddess."

On the ferry, the water blew up into their faces, cold and salty. Amaryllis talked about the history of the island, the sacred land, and the extensive archaeological work that was being done there. CJ's father leaned forward with his elbows on his knees, listening.

Next to Tommy, Tree gripped the base of her seat with one hand and held her hat to her head with the other. Her hair was wet and stringy from the wind, her makeup smeared from the spray. The boat lurched and Tree let go of her hat to steady herself with both hands. In one instant, her hat swept off her head and into the water, where it landed, bobbing along the surface like a chocolate cake.

At the front of the ferry, Amaryllis frowned into her microphone. "Of course," she said, "we try to keep these waters clean."

Tree watched after her hat for a moment, then turned to Tommy miserably. "Do you have sunblock?" she asked, but he had left it on the ship.

Once they reached the island, they walked from site to site along rocky paths. CJ's father stayed up front, close to Amaryllis, while CJ shuffled behind, listening to his Discman. Tree fell to the back of the group, leaning against stone walls and pressing her arms against her hips to keep her skirt from blowing up and exposing her. Her hair swirled around her face, striking her across her eyes and catching in the corners of her mouth. She steadied herself against the wind, her lips pressed together, tight and thin and bloodless as stone.

Finally, Tommy could bear her suffering no longer. He

went to her side and she looked down at him, exhausted and relieved. "Stay up against me, okay?" she asked, and Tommy nodded. For the rest of the tour, he leaned his body into hers, holding down one side of her skirt so that she could hold the other side with her hands. Tommy walked slowly, waiting when she paused to shake a pebble from her shoe. "I feel like crying," she told Tommy.

"I know," he said.

Back on the main island, the group clustered around Amaryllis, dropping tips into her hands. Tommy stood to the side with Tree, his arm circled around her waist, his hip pressing into her hip. Her hair was limp and beaten from the wind, her face and shoulders brightening with a sunburn.

The crowd began to wander away from Amaryllis, but CJ's father continued to talk with her. Finally, Tree told Tommy to remind him that they had to get ready for the formal night.

CJ's father sent Tommy back to Tree with his own message: Tree should take the boys back to the ship and he would follow along shortly. Amaryllis was going to show him a few shops. He had to find something to take back for his sister.

Back in the cabin, Tree showered, then stood in front of the mirror, trying to comb the tangles out of her hair and dabbing makeup over the burn on her cheeks and nose, across her chest and shoulders, into the part of her hair.

"You look really handsome," she said to CJ and Tommy when they were dressed in their tuxedos. She couldn't tie their bow ties, so they wore them loose around their necks while they waited for CJ's father to return. Tommy had not brought dress shoes on the trip—did not own dress shoes—but Tree colored in the white toes of his sneakers with a black marker. "There," she told him, "no one will notice."

When they felt the ship's motors begin to hum beneath

their feet, Tree opened a bottle of wine and poured a glass for herself and another for CJ's father. The ship began to move and Tree sipped from her glass. CJ's father must have stopped for coffee, a drink, a hand at the ship's casino. Ten minutes passed, then twenty. Tree poured herself another glass of wine. CJ's father was probably trying to scare them.

Forty minutes after the ship set sail, they stood on the deck while Tree screamed at a steward that they had to go back. Someone had been left behind. They had to turn the ship around.

Tree's feet were bare, her mouth opening and closing soundlessly as the steward spoke.

Of course, they could not turn the ship around. People got left behind all the time, five or six per cruise. They just caught airplanes to the next port and met up with the ship the next day.

Tommy looked back at the island, white and blue behind them, and half expected to see a figure, small as a toy, waving its arms onshore.

The steward took all of CJ's father's information, then patted Tree's arm and told her not to worry. When people missed the boat, he said, it was often on this island. Mykonos was that sort of place. Lots of friendly people.

When the steward was gone, Tree stood, her mouth parted as she looked out at the water. The makeup she had used to cover her sunburn made her skin look white as clay and her eyes were wide and still. "What if he's hurt?" she asked. "What if he's dead?"

"He isn't dead," CJ said. His eyes were squeezed into slits, his face red and splotchy, his hair dripping sweat into the collar of his tuxedo. "He's with Amaryllis." And Tommy watched as everything inside Tree began to come undone.

Back in the cabin, CJ locked himself in the bathroom and Tree sat on the edge of the bed with her hands pressed between her knees. "I need to be alone for a little while, Tommy," she said. So he took his key and left her there.

Almost everyone on board the ship was in the Main Hall for the formal dinner, and aside from the occasional steward or bellhop, the hallways were empty. Outside the dining room, Tommy could hear the clinks of china and the murmur of laughter and conversation within. After a while, the ship's passengers began to make their way from dinner into the theater, and the hallways clogged with people. They swept against Tommy in a sea of perfume and laughter, their sequined gowns swirling behind them. And then the theater doors closed and the ship was, again, quiet.

As he approached the rear deck, Tommy imagined that he might look back at that island and hear the strained sound of a voice in the distance. "I'm sorry," it would shout. "I want you back!"

But when Tommy reached the rear deck, he saw a red light shining through the glass doors. He pushed them open and the night air swept across his face. The sun had set and in the distance was Mykonos, bright and glistening as a jewel. But above, the sky was filled with a dome of red light so large it stretched from one end of the sea to the other. Tommy stood, petrified.

He felt that he should be afraid, because this was something he had never seen, never heard of, because it was larger than anything he had ever imagined, because it was the sun or a star or a planet full of blood.

But the beauty, bright and full and red as a human heart, made his body ring inside, and he could not be afraid.

Beside him, Tommy heard a voice and realized he was not

alone. A man with thin hair and a curved spine stood in his tuxedo, mouth open, gaping up at the great red sky. "Eighty-eight," he said to Tommy, poking himself in the chest, "and I've never seen that moon before."

And all at once, Tommy knew exactly what the world required of him, what his purpose was, what he was supposed to do. The knowledge filled his head like a song and before he knew what he was doing, he was running back through the ship, down the stairs, through the hallways. Tommy's lungs burned like an engine, the speed pumping through him. Everything had been leading up to this moment, and he thought how the world had worked together to bring him here, how every little piece had played its part—CJ's friends and their fussy mothers, Kemal and the bracelet, CJ's father and Amaryllis. From inside the theater, Tommy could hear the music swelling, cheering him on: Tommy! Tommy! Tommy!

He jammed his key into the lock of their cabin door and burst inside. CJ was still inside the bathroom and Tree was lying on the bed, her mouth open, the bottle of wine empty on the blanket beside her.

"Tree," Tommy said. "Wake up."

She turned her head slightly, and Tommy could see the muddy streaks of her makeup smeared across the pillowcase. A clump of her hair was caught in her mouth, dark with saliva. "I need to show you something," Tommy told her. "Something cool."

He bounced the bed hard with his knee, and when she still wouldn't move, he ran to the bathroom door and pounded with his hands. "CJ! Help me with Tree. You guys have to see the moon!"

"I don't want to see the moon," CJ said from inside the bathroom. "Go away."

Tommy shook Tree and bounced her and shoved her hard with both hands. Then he knelt beside her, pushing her hair off her face. "You have to get up," he whispered. "This is the part where I save you."

But it wasn't to be. She wouldn't wake up. And Tommy went back to the deck alone.

Because he had no other choice, he took the little camera, but even as he walked, he knew that it was useless. The little camera would capture a little moon.

He opened the doors and stepped into the night, and the vastness of that red light washed over him. Again he was struck still in its presence.

The old man had moved on, or Tommy had returned to a different level. The deck was empty. He stood staring up at that great red light over the sea, the immense, lonely mass of it.

But when, at last, Tommy began to cry, it was not because of fear or loneliness or disappointment, but because there was so much beauty, too much beauty for his small body to hold, because some people, most people—his mother and sisters and sweet, pretty Tree, who would never, ever love him, people he had not yet met and strangers he would never know, his father—would live their whole lives and never see this moon, because here he was, only twelve, and already he had seen it.

A Lot Like Fun

For a while, they were all about celebrating. She sold a poem; he sold a book, the movie rights, a second book; she sold another poem, got a job teaching second grade at a ritzy private school where the teachers went to a wine bar after work—*a wine bar*. None of these moments, nor few in between, passed without champagne, without oysters and marijuana and sex three times a day. Another bottle of wine? Another cigarette? Yes, please, they were celebrating!

And then it was over.

He was gone. She was teaching second grade. She was twenty-nine, and she was still smoking. Twenty-nine, her friends told her, was the year it all came down to. If you're still smoking after twenty-nine, they said, you're a smoker.

She thought about quitting the second grade, but everyone agreed that it would be a bad idea. The ritzy school paid health insurance, and she got the summers off. What could be better than that? This was how life went, her friends said. Peaks and valleys. She was in a valley was all.

She stopped reading the books she was supposed to read, the new books, the good books, the books that all her friends were reading. She threw away magazines that covered current events or politics. She quit listening to the radio. "We're on the brink of World War Three," her friends sometimes said, and she would put her head in her arms. "Don't tell me," she begged them. "Please just leave me out of it."

The second grade was something of a comfort. They talked about seasons and birthdays and upcoming holidays. They wrote poems about their pets. The third grade was responsible for teaching multiplication, cursive, and state capitals— the second grade flew beneath the radar. Entire weeks passed in which she never taught a math class. "Practice being nicer people," she told her students for homework. "Watch cartoons," "Eat a cookie," "Ask your parents for a puppy."

At the wine bar after work, there was much talk of *responsibility*: "If we can just teach these kids to be *responsible*," the other teachers would say, "we might be saving the world." *Responsibility* had several subcategories such as personal responsibility, moral responsibility, responsibility to community, and so on. "Shouldn't we learn from the mistakes of our own generation?" the other teachers asked, and she would agree that they should. "How's the writing going?" someone might inquire from time to time, or, "Any new poems coming out soon?" and she would explain how her devotion to the second grade was all-consuming. The other teachers nodded in sympathy: teaching was a full-time life.

This semester, the second grade was supposed to be learning how to tell time and make change. They had cardboard clocks with paper hands, and little baggies of plastic money. She tried a few times, playing make-believe Store so that the children could exchange their plastic money for make-believe groceries. But no one had much fun. After three days, she was sick of it. "Let's color all day," she told her class instead. "Let's order pizza."

Hurray! Hurray! Hurray! In the second grade, she was a superstar, the nicest-smartest-prettiest-coolest teacher ever. They chanted her name and hugged her legs. "Are you lucky to have me?" she asked, and the second grade cheered. When would these children ever need to make change anyway? Their parents were rich. They went to private school. It wasn't like they were going to work in retail when they grew up. "Miss Kelly, what time is it?" one of her students might occasionally ask, and she would hold her palms up: "What time does it *feel* like?"

Her friends thought she needed to get out more. They took her to the movies and to bars. "It's time to pull yourself together," they told her. "It's time to get back on the horse."

They set her up with Mark, who was forty-one, divorced, and working in radio. Most of her friends agreed that Mark was too old for her, but he was a nice guy who sometimes got invited to good parties, and they figured he'd be a fine place to start. "You smoke?" Mark asked the first time they met. "Jesus, I don't know anyone who still smokes."

There were things she liked about Mark: He had good taste in restaurants and knew a few things about wine. Mostly, though, Mark was lonely and not above getting drunk on weeknights. "Do you ever want to get married?" he asked on their second date.

"No," she said, and Mark looked relieved.

Mark had a fifteen-year-old son who lived across town with Mark's ex-wife in Mark's ex-house. The final settlement, Mark told her, had been a bitch. In addition to the house, his ex-wife had kept the car, the dog, and all his skiing equipment, though she herself did not ski. Still, Mark tried to look on the bright side: "She may have kept the house," he said, "but I kept my dignity. And isn't that the most important thing?"

She told him it was. But the next day, she made the second grade vote. "What's the most important thing?" she asked, and they each wrote down an answer. *Chocolate, mothers,* and *Nintendo* were among the most popular answers. *Dignity* didn't even make the top ten.

Most of her students came from broken homes—they seemed to be dealing. Daddies left mommies for girls named Sharon or Melanie and mommies spent too much money and dated men they met at the gym. The second grade came out smelling like a rose, with trips to Disneyland and double Christmases. But Mark was worried about his own son, who, he said, was exceptionally bright and exceptionally sensitive and therefore more at risk for whatever sort of irreversible damage divorce might be capable of inflicting. "He's an artist," Mark told her. "You know the type."

She said she did.

"I thought you might like to meet him," Mark added. "Just in a casual sort of way."

Don't meet the son, her friends said. Kids were not part of the bargain—the last thing she needed. Did she think she was going to marry Mark? Did she think she was going to move in with him or take vacations with him or introduce him to her parents? Well, then.

They made plans to have dinner at her house—Mark would bring his son and she would cook. She was not especially good at cooking, but Mark assured her that his son, being a fifteen-year-old boy, would eat anything. It was going to be great, he said. They would have a quiet little dinner.

They would get to know each other. Mark said that his son was really excited to meet her.

When they showed up at her front door, Mark was beaming like a searchlight. "This is Bernie," he said.

His son stood beside him, pencil-thin, wearing headphones the size of his feet. His cheeks were flushed like he'd been running, and he scowled down at her doormat. "Do you have cable?" Bernie asked without looking at her.

"No," she said, and he turned to his father.

"I hate you."

Leigh made bad decisions—she had been told this her whole life. She had poor instincts when it came to things like directions, ordering from menus, which clothes to pack for which vacations. Now she stood, watching Bernie flip through her CD collection and wondering what she had been thinking when she agreed to this. Sensing he was being watched, Bernie lifted his head. "All these bands suck," he said.

Despite Mark's efforts to keep conversation light during dinner, Bernie glowered over his food and rolled his eyes at every comment his father made. "What's happening in the second grade?" Mark asked.

"I've decided not to teach them how to tell time," Leigh said, and Bernie stabbed his potato with his fork.

"That's fucked-up."

Mark cleared his throat. "Leigh's a creative type," he told his son brightly. "Like you."

Bernie blinked at her, unimpressed. "How can you just not teach them to tell time?"

She took another swallow of wine. "Can you really *teach* someone how to tell time?" she asked, and Bernie squinted.

"Uh, *yeah.*"

"*Time* is man-made," she said, hoping that everyone would finish eating soon so that she could go outside for a cigarette. "It's a conceptual trap. Think of daylight savings," she went on. "Twice a year, we're all supposed to accept that suddenly, we're an hour off. And don't even get me started on the International Date Line."

Bernie turned to his father, a mixture of boredom and disgust curling in his lip. "How long do we have to stay here?"

After that, dinner was pretty much shot. Bernie spent the rest of the evening complaining that the food had given him heartburn, then went home with all the leftovers.

"So," Mark said when he called her later, "you can see what a challenge it is."

"Why did you name him Bernie?" Leigh asked.

"These gifted kids," he went on, "it's like they're always two steps ahead of you."

She had been a gifted kid herself once, had taken the special test and been put in the special class that met three times a week in the Resource Room. Her parents had been thrilled, toasting her with their iced tea at dinner and saying how this was just the beginning, just the first in an endless line of achievements. She was going to have a remarkable life, they told her, filled with remarkable things. In the end, though, the special class was anything but. They met when all the nongifted students were having math class and spent their time drawing pictures of spaceships and writing their own political satires. By the time the year was over, the only difference she could find between herself and the nongifted students was that they had learned fractions and she had not.

"I was hoping we could do this again sometime," Mark said, and she twisted the phone cord around her finger. "This dinner thing with Bernie."

She didn't answer. The first dinner thing had not gone the way she'd imagined it would, though now that she thought back, she realized her imagination had done a pretty piss-poor job: In her fantasy, Mark's son had been pink-cheeked and smelled like powdered sugar. He'd been wearing a corduroy suit. She herself had been wearing high heels and an apron.

She sighed into the receiver. Maybe she should join the Peace Corps.

"The thing is," Mark said after a moment, "the thing is that I'm worried. About Bernie. A little. He's been pretty angry at his mother lately. I'm worried he might not like women."

"Maybe he just doesn't like his mother."

"You're so beautiful," Mark said quietly. "You're so funny."

She closed her eyes. She wanted to be beautiful and funny. "Okay," she said. "We can do it again."

"Leigh writes poetry," Mark told his son during their next dinner, and Bernie stared at her.

"I'm a pretty good poet," he said.

Sometimes you have to toot your own horn, her mother had always told her, but she had always disagreed.

"So," she asked Bernie. "Do you have a girlfriend?"

His mouth puckered. "All the girls I know are cunts."

After dinner, she and Mark went outside to share a cigarette. "Okay," he said, taking a quick drag and turning his head to exhale over his shoulder. "I don't want you to think I'm that dick guy who cares about shit like this, because I swear to God I don't—I *don't care*—but . . ." he took another drag, this one longer, then let his eyes settle on hers ". . . do you think Bernie is gay?"

"No," she said, and Mark exhaled through his nose.

"Really?"

She took her cigarette back and held it to her lips without inhaling. "Gay men are fun."

Her friends told her that joining the Peace Corps was an absurd thing to do. Did she remember the time she decided to run a marathon? The time she wanted to apply for law school? This was no different, another knee-jerk reaction with no foundation in reality. Besides, they said, you had to have *skills* to join the Peace Corps.

"I have skills," Leigh told them, "I can teach," and her friends looked at her like she was wearing a hat with a pinwheel on it.

"My mom thinks I should know more about current events," Elsie Bryant told Leigh while the rest of the second grade clambered out the door for recess. Elsie had pale yellow hair and a small, pink mouth like a wild strawberry against her white skin. Leigh watched Elsie's eyes flicker after her classmates, wishing to join them outside, and wondered if she would be one of those girls who maintained her delicate features as she got older, one of those girls who would grow up to rule the world. Probably, though, Elsie's face would widen and age with the rest of her, her child beauty fading at the moment it began to be useful to her.

"Do *you* think you should know more about current events?" she asked, and Elsie shrugged.

"I don't care."

Elsie would not be in the second grade forever. It was important for her to learn to respect her own needs—was her *mother* going to live her life for her? Besides, Leigh did not expect that she was going to reapply for this job next year. What did she care what Elsie Bryant's mother thought?

At the wine bar after work, she announced her plans to join the Peace Corps and the other teachers applauded. What a wonderful thing to do! So selfless. They bought her drinks and toasted her generosity of spirit—there should be more people like Leigh! She blushed at their attention, but she couldn't help imagining: Maybe she would die heroically, maimed and beaten while fighting injustice, and then someone would write a play about her like they had with what's-her-face.

"Sweetheart," her mother said on the telephone, "are you sure you're thinking this through?"

"Lots of people join the Peace Corps," Leigh told her. "You can't swing a stick these days without knocking over six people who have taught African children about AIDS. *At least.*"

"But aren't they younger?" her mother asked, her voice careful, supportive even through its doubt: *I love you! I believe in you! I want you to be happy!*

"They take people at any age," Leigh explained, "from all walks of life. It says so right on the application."

Her mother was quiet. "What about your job?" she asked finally.

"What about it?"

"You're such a good teacher," her mother said, and Leigh wondered where her mother was getting her information these days, what sort of report card might get sent to her parents regarding her goings-on in the second grade.

"Do you remember when I learned to tell time?" she asked, and her mother paused.

"You were very young."

"How young?"

"I can't remember exactly," her mother confessed. "But it was well before the other children your age, I'd bet my life. You were reading when you were three," she added proudly. "None of our friends could believe it."

"Have you been reading the paper?" Mark asked when he showed up later. She said that she had not. "There's some messed-up shit going on in this town," he told her. "Some seriously messed-up shit."

"Don't tell me."

But he told her. Men were stealing dogs, right out of people's backyards, then cutting their ears off and sealing the wounds with superglue, entering them in dogfights. She covered her own ears with her hands. Could anyone stay quiet about these things? Could anyone, anywhere, just *please* shut the fuck up?

"Sorry," Mark said. "I thought you'd want to know."

What was she supposed to do with this information now that she had it? Should she tell the second grade? This was a current event, after all, the kind of thing that Elsie Bryant's mother wished her daughter was learning about in school. But if it was Leigh's responsibility to pass it on, to strip away their world of cartoons and fairy tales and leave them in this naked, ugly place where men, not monsters, cut the ears off dogs, then made them fight to the death, then she'd rather be in Africa, telling starving children about AIDS. That, at least, was noble.

Over the weekend, Leigh spread the Peace Corps application across her dining room table, then sat staring at it. *Name, address, current occupation.* So far, so good—she had one of each. *Education* was also not an issue. She had a couple of fancy degrees from a couple of fancy colleges. But then came the *experience* section, in which she was supposed to check each box that applied in a list of valuable experiences. *Education/tutoring*? Check. *At-risk youth*? What did that mean, anyway, "at-risk"? Weren't all children at risk in some way or another? Sure, kids who went to private school were probably less likely to join gangs or run away from home and live on the streets. But they'd be able to afford the good drugs when they got older. And let's not forget about eating disorders—already, Leigh noticed the fifth-grade girls in the cafeteria, counting calories and scraping the cheese off their pizza. So, check. *Agriculture*? She'd helped her father in the garden when she was a kid. *Business*? She balanced her own checkbook, filed her own taxes. *Environment*? She recycled. Most of the time. Well, a lot of the time. Check, check, check.

There was a knock at the door, and she turned her application upside down on the table before she went to answer. When she opened the door, Bernie was standing on her porch with his shoulders stooped beneath his backpack. "Is my dad here?"

"No," she told him, and he leaned sideways, peering around her as though she might be lying.

"He's coming here though," he said.

"Later," she told him, and he cleared his throat.

"Can I wait?"

Inside, Bernie opened her refrigerator and stood in front, scowling. There were two bottles of white wine, some salad dressing, a jar of grape jelly. "Is there food?" he asked, and she told him there might be a waffle in the freezer.

Bernie chipped the coat of ice off the waffle with his thumbnail, then tossed it into the microwave without a plate.

When it was finished, he spooned a glob of grape jelly on top, then sat down at the table across from her.

She watched Bernie rip the waffle into quarters, then sop them in jelly and cram them into his mouth with his fingers. She herself had been a pleasant teenager; her parents' friends constantly complimented them on her sweetness, her maturity, her eagerness to please. She had dated wholesome, clear-faced boys who served on the student government and shook her parents' hands on introduction. Bernie's head was low and she could smell his sweat souring in his unwashed hair, could see the dark line of grime beneath his fingernails. He lifted his head and his expression narrowed as he looked at her.

"What kind of poetry do you write?" she asked.

"I write mostly epic poems," Bernie said. "I'm working on one right now about a cyborg. I want something they can make a movie from," he went on. "The real money's in film." He dropped his chin, squinting up at her suspiciously. "Well," he said after a moment, "I probably shouldn't say anything else."

"I know someone whose book is going to be a movie," she said, and Bernie raised one eyebrow doubtfully.

"Yeah?" he asked. "Who?"

She crossed to the bookshelf and Bernie followed. Months had passed since she'd so much as glanced in the direction of her books, and they were coated with a light film of dust. She slid the book from the shelf without looking at it, then dropped it into Bernie's hands. He looked down at the dust and wrinkled his nose. "This is gonna be a movie?"

"Yup."

Bernie flipped through a few pages, then paused on the dedication, reading it silently before holding it up for her to see: *For Leigh, for everything, forever.* "Is this you?" he asked.

"It was."

Bernie stared at her a moment, then read the dedication again. "It says *forever*," he told her.

"There's no such thing."

Bernie closed the book and turned it over, scanning the blurbs on the jacket—*a triumph!*—before handing it back to her. "Could I read some of your poetry?" he asked.

She slid the book back onto the shelf. "No."

Of all the things he had been, he had not been a liar. He'd written those words a long time ago. Probably, when he wrote the word *forever,* he had thought it was the truth. That was the real bitch about time: Everything true would become false, if only you waited long enough.

"This can't last," Leigh told Mark. She couldn't look at his face now without thinking about those earless dogs, the children they'd been stolen from, children who had given them names and slept with them at night. *Mommy, what happened to Pepper? To Midget? To Little Fuzz?* And maybe the parents would be kind enough to lie, to say that they'd been taken by good people who would love them and pet them and feed them scraps from the table.

"What?" Mark asked. "What can't last?"

"This thing with us," she said. "This thing we're doing."

Having sex and getting drunk. Eating dinner with Bernie. Smoking on the porch. She had to quit soon. She was twenty-nine. If she didn't quit soon, the person she was now would be the person she was forever.

"Nothing lasts," Mark said quietly, then cocked his head at her. "Why not?"

"I'm moving to Africa."

"Africa?"

"Well, maybe not Africa," she confessed. "But someplace like Africa."

Mark's forehead creased. "I don't understand," he said. "I thought we were having fun."

"We were," she told him. "We are. It's just . . ."

What? She wasn't bored, not exactly. There were a lot of things she liked about Mark. His jawline smelled like crayons and freshly cut grass. His hands were always clean. At night, he curled his body around her in bed, one arm beneath her neck, the other looped across her waist. She would press herself into the warm weight of him and feel his breath, damp and hot on her throat. And in that foggy place between sleep and waking, he could have been anyone. That was what she liked most about him: In the darkness, he became whomever she wanted.

"You're breaking up with me," Mark said.

"No," she answered. "That's not what I'm doing." Once she turned the application in, it could be several months before the Peace Corps sent her away. What was she supposed to do until then? Sleep alone? Eat alone? Drink wine with the other teachers, then go home alone? There was no reason to break up with Mark. There was no reason to do it right now.

The next day, Bernie showed up at her doorstep again. She worked on her Peace Corps application while he ate the rest of the grape jelly with a spoon and thumbed through the magazines she hadn't thrown away yet.

"Hey," he said, tapping an open magazine. "It's that guy you know."

"What?" Before she could stop herself, she was rising to look.

"He won some big award," Bernie said. Her eyes connected with the photo only an instant before she squeezed
them shut, but there he was, all teeth and stubble. "They're
sending him to Georgia, and Kansas, and Missouri, and—"
She put her hands over her ears and Bernie stopped reading.
"What's wrong?"

"I don't want to know," she said.

"You don't want to know what?" he asked.

"Anything!" she said. "I don't want to know anything about
him. I don't want to know where he is or what he's doing. I
don't want to know that he won some big award." Her face
felt hot, her throat cramped and dry. In another moment,
she would be crying. "I don't want to know that he's going to
Kansas."

Bernie shifted his mouthful of jelly from one cheek to the
other. "Well, he is," he said and looked back down at the
magazine. "He's totally going to Kansas."

Their last night together, she'd cried, held on to his neck, and
she'd begged him not to go. Begged him. When she thought
back on it now, her stomach curled like a worm. She tried
not to remember, tried not to go there, but occasionally, her
memory would make a wrong turn and stumble back on that
moment, and she would be forced to live it again: her weak,
worthless self hanging from him, weeping into his collar, his
body stiff with guilt and misery and resolve, his head turned
sideways so that he wouldn't have to look at her.

If she could have that moment back, she would be stoic,
self-possessed, refined. Maybe then he would have stayed.
Maybe, if she was the type of person who was confident
and self-assured, he would not have fallen out of love with

her. Maybe they never would have found themselves in that moment to begin with.

Stop torturing yourself, her friends said. Stop living in the past. He was gone. Capital G—Gone. He wasn't coming back. She should focus not on the pain, but on the possibility. Something good would come from all this heartache, something always did. Everything, her friends told her, happened for a reason. She should start looking for the silver lining.

She thought she might start looking for new friends.

"You're still working on that?" Bernie asked on the third afternoon that he showed up at Leigh's door. The Peace Corps application was sitting on her table, and though it was only a page long, half the lines remained unfilled. Bernie's face was flushed, his hair damp with rainwater. He stood beside the table, the ratty cuffs of his wet jeans dripping onto the linoleum.

"You can't just throw these things together," she explained. "You have to put some thought into it."

Bernie skimmed over the application. "They're just asking for basic information," he said. "You don't even have to write an essay."

"It's dangerous work," she told him, yanking the application back. "If I don't answer these preliminary questions exactly right, I could end up in the wrong place, with a bag over my head and a knife to my throat."

"I have a cousin in the Peace Corps," Bernie said. "She's in Brazil, teaching blind women how to knit tea cozies."

Leigh scanned the application again. Brazil? Tea cozies? She felt her joints deflate like slashed tires. What was the point in even applying if she would end up so close to home, if she couldn't even put an ocean between herself and this wretched country?

She reached for her purse, digging for her cigarettes while Bernie watched.

"Could I have one?" he asked.

"No."

"I've had them before," he said. "All the time. Most of my friends smoke. It's not like you'd be giving me my first one."

Outside, she cupped her hands around the end of Bernie's cigarette to light it for him, then watched as he inhaled, held the smoke, and let it go. It was true. He'd done it before.

"Why do you want to join the Peace Corps anyway?" he asked. "Aren't you kind of old?"

She lit her own cigarette, then leaned against the railing, exhaling into the rain. "I need a change," she said.

Bernie took another drag, then held his hand out, palm up, letting a few drops of rain plop into it. He examined them for a moment, then licked them off. "Maybe you should get cable."

She watched him smoke and thought, suddenly, that he wasn't bad-looking, or at least that he stood a chance of being not bad-looking when he got older. He had nice skin, nice hair, nice eyes.

"I looked that guy up," Bernie said after a minute. "That guy who wrote the book."

"Don't tell me," she said, and Bernie screwed his mouth to one side.

"There was an interview with him. He sounded like a jerk."

"Really?"

"Totally. He was all, '*Chekhov,* blah, blah, blah,' and '*The postmodern predicament,* blah, blah, blah.' And I was like, *What an asshole.*"

"He was always a horn tooter," she agreed.

"When did you break up?" Bernie asked.

"A while ago."

Bernie reached for another cigarette and she didn't move to stop him. "Who left who?" he asked.

"*Whom,*" she said.

Bernie waited while she lit his second cigarette, then leaned back against the porch rail, watching her. "He did," she said finally. "He left me."

"How come?"

Because she wasn't smart enough, wasn't pretty enough, wasn't funny enough. Because she was needy and weak and left her dirty clothes in piles rather than putting them in the hamper. Because she was a person who could not, might not ever, get her life together. Because she was not good enough for him.

"He met someone he liked better," she said.

"Are you still in love with him?"

"Yes."

Bernie stubbed his cigarette out on the bottom of his shoe and threw the butt into the yard. He started toward the door, then paused with his hand on the knob and turned back to her. The rain was falling in sheets around them, the air pinched with cold. "Then what are you doing with my dad?"

Through the exhalation of her cigarette smoke, she saw the slight tremble of chill in the rails of Bernie's arms, the open, endless place of waiting inside of him.

"I'm killing time."

Bernie nodded slightly, his mouth pulling sideways as he considered this. For a moment, she thought he might start laughing. But then his gaze dropped, his expression darkening into its familiar scowl. "You should get cable," he said again, then went inside, closing the door behind him.

The next night, Mark took her out for dinner. "I've been thinking," he said, "about what you said the other night, about things not lasting."

Leigh tried to smile. "I think I was drunk then," she said. She'd wanted it to come out funny, but the words were slurred and clumsy. When wasn't she drunk?

"I've been talking to Bernie," he went on.

"Did you know he smokes?"

"I think we should call things off," Mark said. "Before someone gets hurt."

She closed her eyes.

"You're going to Africa," he said. "We'd have to end it then anyway."

She thought of the Peace Corps application, still sitting on her table, still half-finished. She nodded.

"It's been fun," Mark told her. "I mean, really, a lot of fun."

"We can still be friends," she said, and Mark patted her on the hand.

"Sure," he said. "Sure we can."

Good riddance, her friends said. *Adios*. Mark was too old for her anyway. They had nothing in common. She was young! In the prime of her life! Really, she was lucky that Mark had ended it when he had, before she got attached. Leigh was a catch-and-a-half, they said. Someday, the right guy was going to come along, the guy who would sweep her off her feet and treat her like gold. All good things to those who wait, they said. Leigh just needed to have patience. She needed to have faith.

"Does anyone know what time it is?" she asked, and the second grade stared at her, confused. Of course they didn't know. "It's eleven-eleven," she told them and stood on a chair to point at the hands of the clock. They turned in their seats to watch.

"Eleven-eleven is a magical minute," she went on. "It's the minute when you can make a wish."

The second grade seemed skeptical, but she made them set down their crayons and markers, made them close their eyes. "Wish hard," she said. "Keep wishing."

When the minute was up, she let her students open their eyes and they blinked, their lashes damp from the force of their wishing. Leigh climbed down from the chair. Eleven-twelve, eleven-thirteen, eleven-fourteen—she didn't bother the second grade with these ordinary minutes. By now the class had returned to the private continents of their drawings, and Leigh moved between their desks, peeking over their shoulders into their worlds of silver-winged mermaids and chocolate cupcake trees and happy stick families holding hands on front porches.

Company of Strangers

The only thing my brother and I ever agreed on was that I would die horribly. As a child, I knew that I could be trapped in a tanning bed until my skin bubbled and melted away from my skeleton. I could be swallowed by an earthquake, washed away in a flash flood, eaten alive by rats. I could spontaneously burst into flames or choke to death on a Cheerio. I could catch the Ebola virus and bleed to death from my eyes and nipples.

Our father failed to recognize the seriousness of my impending death. A doctor, he saw only the facts: "Monkeys get Ebola, floods don't hit the suburbs, and rats are just squirrels with naked tails."

"Maybe I'll be kidnapped," I told my father. "On any ordinary day, I could get stolen and chopped into little pieces."

He sighed heavily and looked at me over the rim of his glasses. "By whom?"

"By bad men," I told him and pointed at my brother. "It could happen. Jack said."

My father glared at my brother, who nodded. "It's true. She could."

Bad men were everywhere. They filled the pages of newspapers and monopolized the Six O'Clock News. It was only a matter of time before one came through my window at night and snatched me from my canopy bed. He would bruise my arms, pull my hair, tear my nightgown. A bad man could fill a child's mouth with one fist to keep her from screaming, could duct-tape her hands behind her back, could slice her apart and throw her into a river.

"I could be gone in a heartbeat," I told my father. "And maybe all the police would ever find is a finger." I wagged my pinkie in front of him. "Better take a good look in case you ever have to identify me by it."

My father took a deep breath. "Let's not worry about it, shall we? You just be good and safe and remember what they told you in school about talking to strangers."

"It isn't always a stranger," my brother interrupted. "One of our neighbors could lock Lilly up in a cellar and take pictures of her without her clothes on."

"That will never happen," my father told me. "But if it does, I will save you." Then he cuffed my brother on the back of the head and hissed, "For the love of God, Jackson, please don't make my life any harder than it already is."

My father's wife had died young. His job was demanding. His son was cold and his daughter walked home from school ready to accept candy from the first stranger who offered. The women he might have hoped to love moved through his house like a parade, smoked cigarettes in his kitchen, then fled the first time they met his children. They left for good when his son looked them up and down and whispered "Whore" beneath his breath. They ran from the house screaming when his daughter smeared lipstick across her neck and wrists and lay naked in the bathtub the first time they tried to spend the night. My father's life *was* hard. But this was something my brother and I did not agree on.

When my father died, my brother flew into town to stand with me at his bedside and watch him draw his last breaths. I held my father's hand and thought about how he would never kneel beside my coffin or cry over my tombstone, while Jack used the hospital phone to rearrange meetings and cancel appointments.

"I hope he doesn't drag this out," my brother said between calls. "The kids are missing school."

In the hallway his wife read magazines while his children made trips to the vending machine on the first floor. When I passed by them to go to the bathroom, they stared at me like I was something from a fairy tale: a unicorn, a hunchback, a three-headed dog, something they'd read about in books but never thought they'd see in real life. I knew my brother's family only from the annual Christmas cards my father forwarded to me, photos of the four of them engaging in festive activities, wearing matching holiday sweaters and smiling like a family made by Fisher-Price.

After my father had taken his last breath, I stood in the hallway with my niece and nephew while my brother held his wife's elbow and whispered into her ear. "We'll deal with formalities," he said when he turned back to me. He tossed me my father's car keys. "You keep the kids busy for a while."

My sister-in-law made a face like she'd been struck by lightning. "Jack," she said in a strained voice, and he touched her shoulder.

"Just for a couple of hours," he told her, then smiled at me. "Shouldn't I help?" I asked.

"Ann and I will make sense of things," he said. "The sooner we get through this mess, the sooner we can all get the hell out of here." He put his hand on his son's head. "The kids have spent all day in the hospital. They're restless." He checked his watch and filled my hand with bills from his wallet. "It will be much easier this way."

I pretended not to notice as Ann slipped some money to her daughter and whispered, "Just in case." She followed us to the elevator, clapping her hands gaily as she called after her children, "Emma? James? Seat belts!"

I looked down at my niece and nephew. "What do you want me to do with them?" I asked Jack. "Where should we go?"

He handed me a newspaper from a chair in the hallway. "Take them to a museum or something. Art show, historical exhibit, I don't care. Just do something cultural."

We had to drive thirty minutes to get to the pirate dinner theater. Emma played navigator with a map she found in the glove compartment. I turned when she told me to and smoked the cigarettes she'd found underneath the map. From the backseat, James tapped my shoulder several times a minute to remind me that he had to go to the bathroom.

Emma turned in her seat. "You'll just have to hold it," she told her brother. "I don't think it would be a good idea to stop in this neighborhood." Then she lowered her voice and gave me a sideways glance. "It looks *unsanitary*."

We bought our tickets from a woman wearing corduroy pants and an eye patch who told us that we were prisoners of the Yellow Pirate and to go on over to our table.

Once we were seated, Emma—who thanks to her father has a sense of such things—looked around at the cardboard anchors taped to the walls and said, "I have a feeling that this is going to be terribly overpriced."

"You can't put a price on culture," I told her.

James rolled his eyes. "*You* can't," he said. "It's *Daddy's* money."

"He wanted to pay," I said. "But I could have if I'd wanted to. I have money, you know."

Emma narrowed her eyes at me. "Do you have a *job*, Aunt Lilly?"

I narrowed my eyes back. "Do *you*?"

She leaned forward in her seat. "I'm eleven."

"You shouldn't think of excuses to fail," I told her. "You should think of reasons to succeed." Her forehead wrinkled and she looked at her brother, who cranked his finger beside his temple and mouthed the word *crazy*.

"For your information," I said, "I have had *many* jobs. Most recently, I worked for the Red Cross in rescue relief." Emma's mouth pulled to the side doubtfully. "That's right," I told her. "Anytime there was a natural disaster, they called me and off I went to be right in the middle of it. It was a great job."

I didn't tell them that the job was volunteer. The only person who knew that had been my father, who had groaned into the phone and asked to what address he should send a monthly check.

"You don't need to send money," I'd told him. "This is very dangerous work. Chances are that I'll be dead within the month." When he didn't answer, I gave him the address of Red Cross headquarters and told him that they would be able to forward my mail.

"So?" James asked. "How come you're not doing it anymore if it was such a great job?"

"Well," I said. "Sadly enough, it turned out that I didn't have any skills. Everyone else on my team could do important things like CPR or lift fallen buildings off of orphaned children." I ignored the glance exchanged between them. "I did what I could, though. I held up signs and handed out snack packs to the devastated."

The Yellow Pirate came to our table with chips and salsa. He was small and thin with a black goatee penciled onto his chin and a yellow scarf tied around his head. After a great deal of grimacing and *argh*-ing, he took our drink orders and told us that he would make us walk the plank if we didn't behave. "You especially," he added, wagging his finger at me. "I can tell you're trouble." James snorted and Emma leaned her head against her hands. "Wow," the Yellow Pirate said, looking us over. "Who died?"

"Our grandfather," James told him. "But no one really liked him much, so it's okay." The Yellow Pirate stared for a second and then took a step backward.

"You know what this table needs?" he asked. "This table needs to see my sword." Emma yawned audibly and the Yellow Pirate leaned down and whispered to her, "This is a big deal. You'll have to keep it quiet so that the other tables don't get jealous." He winked at me. "I don't show my sword to just anybody."

"Oh," I said. "I bet you say that to *all* the tables."

He made a great show of brandishing the sword before us, swishing it over our heads and growling for effect.

"It's really big," I said. "Can I touch it?" He set the gray plastic against the inside of my arm, and I ran my finger along the edge. "I bet you can do some real damage with that." I slid my foot from under the table and pressed it over the toe of his shoe.

"See?" he said to me. "I could tell right away about you." Before he moved sideways to the next table, he reached down and touched the backs of his fingers to my hair.

When I looked up, James was staring at me. "My dad isn't going to like that you brought us here."

"Your dad can bite me," I told him, and his mouth fell open.

"It's all right," Emma said nervously and patted her brother's arm. "She doesn't know what she's saying. She's *bereft*. Aren't you, Aunt Lilly?"

I thought of Jackson across town, smoking a cigar and cursing to himself as he leafed through our father's papers, through his receipts and tax returns and letters, things he never meant for us to see. "That's right," I told them and slipped on my complimentary eye patch. "I'm all torn up inside."

"Daddy says that Grandpa was a bad man," James said. He glanced behind him and lowered his voice. "Daddy says that Grandpa had girlfriends and it broke Grandma's heart so bad it killed her."

I lifted my eye patch to look at him. "That's why *Daddy* is a lawyer instead of a doctor," I told him. "*Cancer* killed Grandma. Check the records if you don't believe me."

Emma was loading a chip with salsa and she stopped midway to her mouth. "When you and Dad were little?"

"That's right," I said.

"What did you do?"

The pirates were gathering onstage and I folded my napkin across my lap. "Well," I said. "Once I dug my knee back and forth on the sidewalk in front of our house. It bled so much that the cement turned pink and Jack had to bandage me up with dish towels and masking tape."

"Did he cry?"

"Nah," I said. "He was pretty used to it."

"No." Emma dropped her chip back into the bowl and put her hands flat on the table. "When Grandma died. Did my dad cry?"

"Oh." I stared at the stage, hoping something would happen. "I don't remember."

It was your basic pirate-dinner-theater scenario. There were two main pirates (the Yellow Pirate turned out to be a marginal pirate figure) and two captured princesses: a gypsy princess and a princess-princess. After various failed escapes, the princesses ended up falling in love with their respective pirates and in between our fish sticks and our ice cream sandwiches, the whole ensemble did a big dance number while the gypsy princess turned a series of backflips across the stage.

Sometime during the curtain call, James lost his shoe under the table and the rest of the audience filed out around us while I scouted on my hands and knees to find it. The cast was lingering in the auditorium, eating chips from abandoned bowls and clearing plates away in plastic bins.

As James was cramming his shoe back onto his foot, the Yellow Pirate sat down on our table and crossed his arms.

"So," I said to him. "Have you always wanted to be a pirate?"

He cocked his jaw. "Where are you going now?" he asked.

"We're going back to our hotel," Emma said and gave me a firm look. "Mom and Dad are *expecting* us."

The Yellow Pirate kept his eyes on mine. "I think you should come to my place."

"I have the kids," I said, and he poked my hip with his sword.

"I have a TV."

At the hotel there would be polite conversation. Jack and Ann would talk about their jobs, their kids, their friends. They would talk about the things they'd found in my father's house, and I would sit like a stranger between them while they picked a church and planned a funeral.

I handed my father's car keys to the Yellow Pirate. "We can take our car," I said. "You drive."

As we walked across the empty parking lot, James tugged at the hem of my shirt. "I want to go, Aunt Lilly. I'm hungry."

"You should have eaten your dinner," I told him.

He wrinkled his nose. "My fish sticks tasted like refrigerator."

Emma nodded. "Mine were frozen in the middle."

The Yellow Pirate started my father's car, and I guided James and Emma to the backseat. "We'll stop for food," I promised. "Just get in." I held the door open and Emma took a step backward.

"I think this is a very bad idea," she said and folded her arms over her chest.

"Well, guess what?" I asked her. "I couldn't care less what you think." As soon as I said it, I tried to smile, to make it a joke, but her lips froze and her face emptied. She swallowed hard and dropped her chin to her chest as she followed her brother into the backseat.

The Yellow Pirate lived in an apartment with stained walls

and concrete floors. In the doorway, James reached for my hand. "Aunt Lilly," he whispered with his mouth trembling. "I want my mom."

"Soon," I told him and shook his hand away. The Yellow Pirate turned on the television, and James and Emma stood awkwardly in front of it, looking around at the piles of clothes and empty beer bottles while the Yellow Pirate touched his lips to my neck and breathed into my ear. I slid my fingers into the waist of his pants, and over his shoulder, I saw Emma watching. Her face was empty, and our eyes locked for a moment before she turned away. "Wait here," I said. "We'll just be a minute."

He didn't tell me his name and I didn't ask. In the bedroom, he shed his pirate garb in a heap on the floor and stood before me with thin arms and a narrow, hairless chest. We lay on his bed, a mattress on the floor next to the water heater, and he ran the palm of his hand up my shin and stopped at my knee.

"Nasty scar," he said, and I looked down. He traced the patch of pink scar tissue with his index finger and smiled. "Did you get it doing something brave?"

I closed my eyes. "I rubbed it on concrete until I saw bone." His hand fell away from my leg and I tried not to smile. But when I opened my eyes, he wasn't gaping in horror. His mouth was twitching and his chest was rising and falling in quick, shallow breaths.

"Jesus Christ," he said into his hand. "You're a masochist."

Without the scarf and sword, he had lost a good deal of his mystique. His goatee had smeared up the side of his face like a giant bruise and his hair smelled like sweat and fish sticks. The lights were too bright and I wanted to get up, to get dressed, to get out. But his little face looked so excited.

After all his pirate work, his singing/dancing/table waiting, it seemed rude to disappoint him. "I guess so," I said.

"Oh God." He jumped off the bed and began rummaging through his dresser drawers. "I've done that show, like, a million times and nothing like this has ever happened!" He turned back to me with a pair of furry rings dangling from his thumb. "Check it out," he said and shook them in front of me when I didn't respond. "They're handcuffs."

"They're pink," I said.

"Yeah," he nodded. "Pink. You know, for girls?"

I let him move my hands behind my head and snap my wrists to the pipes of the water heater. The television murmured from the other room and I turned my head to the side so that I wouldn't see the Yellow Pirate's goatee smear onto my skin.

Jack would have finished with my father's house. He and Ann would have had a nice dinner in our nice hotel and they would be counting the hours until they could fly back to their nice home with their nice family. We would put my father into the ground and then they would be gone. They would reappear on the faces of future Christmas cards smiling and laughing as they decorated a tree, sat in front of a fireplace, posed on cross-country skis, cards full of matching outfits and warm wishes, cards I would never see. *From our family to yours.* No one would ask what address to mail them to.

It would have been an easy escape. No police bursting through the door with guns outstretched. No spot on the Six O'Clock News. No father swinging in like the Phantom of the Opera to save me. The pink handcuffs had a self-release button. And the Yellow Pirate didn't try to stop me.

The living room looked the same, cluttered with empty pizza boxes and dirty dishes. But my niece and nephew were not in it. The lights were on and the TV hummed in the corner. We looked in the kitchen, in the bathroom. We crawled on our hands and knees to look under the furniture. We looked in closets and cabinets and behind doors. "Enough hiding," I called. "Emma? James? Come out now. Aunt Lilly doesn't want to have to beat the hell out of you!" I listened for the sound of voices, of rustling, of breathing. Nothing.

"I'm sure they didn't go far," the Yellow Pirate said when I went onto the porch. "I'll help you find them. Just let me get dressed." I left him there and ran into the street. There was no traffic, no light, no children. I checked inside the car, but there was no movement, no sound, no children. I yelled their names, then screamed them. I stood in the center of the road, trying to be logical. If I was a kid, which way would I go? In which direction would I run to escape the lair of the Yellow Pirate, to get home, to get safe, to leave me behind?

There are rules for crises, codes for danger: Starve a fever; feed a cold; stop, drop, and roll; stay with a buddy. But there was nothing useful. So I ran. I circled one block and then the next, calling their names until my voice went hoarse and the words fell dull and dead in my mouth. Until I couldn't remember which street I'd been down or which direction I'd come from. I passed three pay phones, or maybe one pay phone three times, and each time I did, I thought about calling the hotel. They might have gone back, might be in the arms of their parents, explaining the horrors that had driven them to venture alone into the night, into the cold, into a city they didn't know. I held the receiver in my hand and let my fingers shake over the keys. In the face of danger, what were you supposed to do? Call 911. Kick and yell. Scream *fire*. Scream *rape*. Make a scene. *This is not my father!*

But if they were back, then they were fine. And if they weren't . . . I hung up the phone.

I circled blocks of dark buildings and empty streets until I found myself at my father's car, back in front of the Yellow Pirate's apartment, where I sat down on the curb and let my feet sink in the gutter mud. I smoked my father's cigarettes with fingers numb from cold and stared at the dark sky. Around me, the city stretched into state, into country, into a whole world of strangers. The sphere of the earth was crowded with people who would never know me, would never look for me, would never try to find me if I disappeared. I wrapped my arms around my knees. A person is missing only if another person misses them.

I smoked and waited. I waited for hypothermia or lung cancer or morning. *Stay where you are and someone will find you*. And someone did. I heard a door open behind me and the Yellow Pirate came out of his apartment with James and Emma on either side.

"Where have you been?" he asked. "I told you they didn't go far." They stood, the three of them, silhouetted in the light of his doorway.

"Where?" I said and tried to stand. But my ankles were numb and my legs felt stiff and heavy.

"Burger King around the corner." They moved down the steps and into the street in front of me. "They'd said they were hungry."

Emma was chewing on the straw of her paper cup. "We were hungry," she confirmed. "You said we'd get food and we didn't and we were hungry."

The Yellow Pirate helped me to the car and held the back door open for James and Emma. "Come see the show again," he said, and I nodded mutely. "Bring your friends."

I drove the car down the street, the same street I'd walked, but it didn't look familiar. "I don't know where we are," I said. Emma didn't offer to help with the map, so I just drove, working my hands around the steering wheel as the feeling came back into my fingers. In the backseat, James's body slumped sideways into sleep while Emma sat rigid, staring out the window and squeaking the straw in the lid of her cup.

"Some night," I said finally.

"Yeah," she said. "Some night."

"You know," I told her, "maybe we shouldn't tell your parents everything that happened tonight." The squeaking stopped.

"Are you saying to lie?" she asked. "We should lie to Mom and Dad?"

"No," I said quickly. "It's just that sometimes, the truth makes people upset. And it doesn't do any good to make people upset. So maybe we could avoid the truth. Just a little bit."

"Aunt Lilly," she said slowly. "That's the exact same thing as lying."

"No, it isn't," I told her. "It's like, when someone asks you how you are and even though you want to say that you feel like shit, that you're miserable, that you cry until you gag and spend most of your time imagining ways to kill yourself, instead you just say, 'Fine, thanks.'"

"I don't think it's like that at all," she said. "I think that's just good *manners*."

The car was quiet for a moment and then I heard the sound of Emma's seat belt unhooking. There was a rustling noise and she was beside me, leaning between the two front seats. She touched my arm lightly. "Aunt Lilly?" she asked. "Are you miserable? Do you think about killing yourself?"

"Of course not." I tried to laugh. "I was just using that as a *for instance*."

"Oh." She touched the side of her face to my arm. "How was the Yellow Pirate?" she asked, and I glanced down to see if she meant something by it. But her eyes were half-closed and her face looked soft.

"Kind of boring," I said, and she nodded as if she'd suspected as much.

"Your voice is scratchy," she said. "Have you been crying?"

"My throat's just dry," I told her.

She climbed into the front and I put my hand on her back to steady her as she crawled into the passenger seat. "It's mostly ice," she told me and held out her soda cup. "But there's a little left." I reached out to take it and she touched her hand against mine on the cup. "Hey," she said. "Our fingers are the same."

I glanced down at our hands, at our square knuckles and oval nails. "How about that," I said.

She squeezed my finger and pointed ahead. "Turn here."

When we got to the hotel, James wouldn't wake up, and I had to carry him across the parking lot by one armpit and the crook of one knee, hiking him up by his clothes when he slipped. My brother and his wife were alone in the hotel lobby, pacing in front of the desk. Their heads snapped toward us when we walked through the front doors and my brother dropped his chin to his chest and exhaled slowly. Ann ran forward and snatched James from my arms, pulling his head to her shoulder and his legs around her waist. Her eyelashes were wet, and I could see the veins throbbing in her neck as she kissed James's ear and touched her hand to Emma's hair.

She wrapped both arms around James and rocked him back and forth, whispering, "My God, my God."

When she looked at me, her lip was quivering and her mouth opened and closed with each jagged breath.

"Well," she said finally. "Don't you have *anything* to say?"

Next to her, Emma's body jerked like the question had been directed to her. "Thank you, Aunt Lilly," she said politely. "We had a very nice time."

Ann looked at the carpet and held one hand up to Jack. "I'll be up in a minute," he told her, and she gave me a narrow stare before taking her children into the elevator.

When we were alone, Jackson stood in front of me with his hands in his pockets and his jaw flexing. "Well, Lilly," he said. "Ann hates you now."

"She hated me before," I told him. "I've just given her an excuse to say so."

He leaned toward me and sniffed. "What's that I smell on you?" he asked, and I shrugged.

"Pirate?"

"It's cigarette smoke," he said. "You've been smoking in front of my kids." He closed his eyes and shook his head. "God, Lilly."

"I've had a rough night," I told him, and he held his hands up.

"I can't do this now," he said. "I'll talk to you tomorrow."

"Wait," I said and caught the sleeve of his shirt. "I thought we could talk a little bit, get a drink or something."

He stared at my hand on his arm until I let it drop. "The bar closed an hour ago," he said and stepped into the elevator.

"Just for a minute, Jack. Please." I pressed the heels of my hands into my eyes to stop them from burning and swallowed hard to release the tightening in the back of my throat. "I've had a really terrible night."

Jack's face went hard, and as the elevator door began to close, his hand slammed out and held it open. "Let's hear it, Lilly," he said through the clench of his jaw. "Give me one reason. Just one reason why I should feel sorry for you."

My whole body felt weak and hollow, like in one moment it might forget how to move, how to stand, how to breathe. I touched my fingers to my lips in the hope that they would remember my voice and say something, say anything. "My father died today."

Jack watched me for a moment. He blinked several times, then looked up at the ceiling and laughed. He pulled his shirtsleeve up and lifted his wrist so that I could see the face of his watch. Then the doors closed between us and he was gone. The hours had crossed over the day my father died. And I was standing in a hotel lobby on just an ordinary day.

Take Care

The summer before Kate's sister dropped out of college, they both got jobs working for a dentist. Kate was sixteen and had been sent to stay with Claudia in Claudia's college apartment while their parents figured a few things out, including whether or not they wanted to stay married to each other (not) and how much larger their kitchen should be (much), though probably not in that order.

Up until now, Kate had never spent much time with her sister, mostly because Claudia was five years older and had always existed largely outside the boundaries of Kate's world, but also because Claudia found Kate annoying. "You could be twins," people often said to them, and it was almost true. They had the same dark, shaggy hair and ghostly skin, the same narrow jaws and thin, bloodless lips, the same long, creepy fingers. But Claudia was taller and thinner. Not enough to keep people from mistaking them for each other when they ran into them alone. But enough that—so long as they were together—no one ever got them confused.

They were terribly unhappy that summer, Claudia because she was doing poorly in school; because she thought that their parents were overbearing tyrants who had never understood her; because she felt pent-up and pushed-around; because she had fallen in love again; and because, again, the experience had not gone well. Kate was terribly unhappy because she was always terribly unhappy.

Originally, the plan had called for Kate to spend the summer in New Hampshire with an aunt. Kate had not cared for this plan, but her parents made great promises—spend the summer in New Hampshire, they told her, and in the fall she could have her own phone line, an extended curfew, and limitless use of the car. Kate rarely got phone calls or invitations to go out, and she had yet to learn how to drive, but she liked the idea of herself as someone who could benefit from such a bargain, and so she agreed to it.

In school, Kate read novels about girls who were kleptomaniacs or drug addicts or in love with their brothers, and the absence of such suffering in her own life was a source of perpetual anguish to her. Kate's unhappiness was like weather, a storm rolling constantly toward or away from her, a force she could feel approaching like a hum of electrical current across her skin before it broke open, soaking her in sadness, and she would have no choice but to brace against the misery until it wore itself out on her and passed on to someone else.

How she longed for a tragedy—a well in which to pour her sorrow—a rare blood disease or psychotic break, a doomed love affair, one in which many people would be invested and many people would get hurt. It was her great hope that something god-awful might happen in New Hampshire.

But two weeks before Kate was to leave, Claudia told a TA

that she was going to kill herself, then stabbed a pair of scissors into the back of her hand. And after that, the summer belonged to Claudia.

What their father didn't have time for, he explained as he drove Kate the three hours north to Claudia's, was this bullshit with the college. After the incident with the scissors, Claudia had not been permitted to finish the semester and was required to meet with a psychologist at the Student Health Center once a week for the whole summer. If at the end of the summer this psychologist gave her approval, Claudia would be welcome back to school in the fall.

Mountains from molehills, Kate's father said. This was a college, for Christ's sake. If they got rid of every high-strung girl who dabbled in the art of self-mutilation, there wouldn't be a single female left on campus. And that included faculty.

This mess was because of a professor, that's what Kate's father said, another married man with loose morals with whom Claudia had managed to entangle herself. Things fell apart, of course, then so did Claudia. When she couldn't find the professor, she went to his TA—some poor kid grading papers who nearly shit his pants when Claudia skewered herself in his cubicle.

"Who's the professor?" Kate asked, and her father squinted for a moment as if he was about to sneeze, then didn't.

The details, he said, were unimportant. Besides, that was all over. And the college didn't know a thing about the relationship—the college didn't need to know. From here on out they would handle the situation as a family, and as a family, their focus should be keeping Claudia on the right track.

Kate's father knew that he was asking a lot of her, knew

that he had made certain promises in return for her compliance in spending the summer in New Hampshire, and he was willing to uphold those promises even though New Hampshire was no longer part of the bargain. He was, in fact, willing to up the ante. All Kate had to do was help keep her sister out of trouble this summer and her father would, upon Kate's graduation from college in six years, give her the down payment on a house. Now, how about that for a deal?

Kate worried that Claudia would not approve of this arrangement. But the night their father delivered Kate to her sister's apartment, Claudia threw her arms around Kate's neck and buried her face in her shoulder. Claudia's hair smelled like marijuana and cigarette smoke and Kate could feel the angles of her body through her clothing, all edges and corners and knobs. "Thank God you're here," Claudia said. "I've been so fucked-up and lonely."

Growing up, Claudia had never taken the slightest notice of Kate, but now she clung to her. She wound her fingers through Kate's hair and leaned sideways against her when they watched television. The affair with the professor, Claudia said, had left her broken and wasted and useless. They sat on Claudia's futon, and Claudia rested her head on Kate's thigh as she talked about her heartbreak, her misery, her feelings of desperation. She hadn't really wanted to kill herself, she said. She'd only wanted word to get back to him that she'd tried.

Kate looked down at the bandage on the back of Claudia's hand, a square piece of gauze held in place by several rows of white tape. Claudia's heart had been raped and pillaged for the last time, she said. Men were savages, every single one of them, and she vowed that she was done with them forever. Besides, Claudia had Kate now. They would look after each other, would guard each other from the outside world and stave off each other's loneliness. All they had to do was make it through the next six years, Claudia said, and then they could live in the house Kate's father had promised her.

Kate pictured their lives stretching beyond them like an endless summer, the house, which could be any house, full of Claudia's things—Claudia's pictures and futon and wall tapestries that smelled like incense, her twinkle lights and cinder-block bookshelves—the house where they would grow old and forget the world together.

At night, Claudia begged Kate to sleep in her bed with her—"Don't leave me alone," she whispered, "I can't bear to sleep alone"—and Kate had never felt more loved.

The day before Claudia was to meet with her psychologist, she made a plea to Kate: Hadn't she been through enough? Her heart was broken, she'd been kicked out of school, and now she was supposed to talk to a stranger about it? Claudia was sure the psychologist wouldn't notice if—just for this week—Kate went in her place.

"What will I talk about?" Kate asked, and Claudia said she didn't care.

"Whatever you want. Talk about me. I've told you everything. You tell her, then tell me what she says."

A flutter of panic stirred through Kate's stomach. "What if I mess up?"

Claudia frowned. "Then I'll hate you."

The next morning, Claudia taped a piece of gauze across the back of Kate's hand, then stood so that they could examine each other side by side in the bathroom mirror. Just think,

Claudia said after a moment, if Kate lost five pounds and Claudia gained five, they'd look exactly the same.

Claudia didn't want to risk being seen together, so Kate walked the eight blocks to the college by herself, then waited at the Student Health Center for Claudia's name to be called. The session was not nearly as difficult as Kate had feared. Claudia's psychologist asked what was going on in Claudia's life, and Kate told her about Claudia's professor, how they had met in a bar and he had bought her a drink because he was alone and she was crying. The two had fallen in love, had been meant to fall in love by some great force that might or might not be God. Claudia had thought everything was going to be different now, that because he loved her, her life would change. But then he stopped coming to see her. He stopped returning her calls. At the end of the hour, Kate walked home and told Claudia that her psychologist thought she was very brave.

Claudia was delighted. She cupped her hands around Kate's face and kissed her forehead. "You'll go from now on."

During the day, Claudia and Kate stayed inside, smoking cigarettes and watching miniseries after miniseries about long-suffering daughters of plantation owners who, in spite of having riches and beauty beyond compare, were miserable because they loved men they could not be with. These men were usually poor or black or away at war. Sometimes they were scoundrels. "I am terribly unhappy," Claudia and Kate said to each other in their best Southern belle accents. "I was born to *suffah*."

The second time Kate went to Claudia's psychologist, they talked about how Claudia spent her time. "I watch television," Kate said. "I cry in bed. And I smoke a lot of pot." Then she went home to deliver the news: They had to get jobs.

Claudia laughed. "Forget it."

But the following week, Claudia's psychologist was more insistent—Claudia was not to spend the summer smoking pot and watching television. Claudia needed to dress up and go out. She needed to be counted on to do set tasks, then rewarded for doing these tasks. Getting a job, Claudia's psychologist said to Kate, was going to make all the difference in improving Claudia's chances of functioning successfully in the larger world. Then she called Kate's father and said the same thing to him.

The dentist needed someone who could start right away, and the work was not skilled—answering phones and mailing letters. His office was in a large building filled with different doctors' offices: dermatologists and optometrists, other dentists. Claudia and Kate sat in a row of chairs with two other women who were also waiting to interview. The other women were older and heavier and they both wore shapeless floral dresses and panty hose. Claudia thumbed through a fashion magazine while they waited, and Kate nudged her wrist, then gestured toward the women. *Should we have worn panty hose?* she mouthed. Claudia looked at their legs, then shook her head no.

The dentist had broad shoulders and square hands and hair so yellow Kate thought it must be dyed. During their interview, he looked over their résumés, which were not really résumés but lists of clubs they'd belonged to in high school and awards they'd won in activities like track and choir. The dentist had a deep voice and a thick, scruffy mustache, which Claudia would later say was proof that his hair color was natural, because what kind of person would dye a mustache?

"So," the dentist asked them, "what do you want to be when you grow up?"

"Journalists," Kate said, because she thought this would

make him want to hire them to answer his phone and mail his letters.

"Millionaires," Claudia said, and the corner of his mustache twitched.

He asked why they wanted to work in his office, and Claudia told him that dentists gave beautiful smiles to people who might not otherwise have them and that they both admired this service, though they themselves had inherited perfect teeth and never needed braces.

They smiled then so that he could see their perfect teeth, and the dentist rocked back in his chair, folding his fingers beneath his chin. Orthodontists, he said, were responsible for braces. Not dentists.

Kate tried to think of something interesting she knew about dentists to prove that they thought dentists were interesting, but before she could come up with anything, Claudia leaned forward, resting her elbows lightly on the dentist's desk. Also, she said, they had perfect vision.

The dentist had not been planning to hire two people—there was hardly enough work for one—but he wanted his practice to have a warm, family feeling, and what better way than to hire sisters? People would know right away Claudia and Kate were sisters, he said, because he himself had known right away. Some might even think they were twins!

The snag, he told them, had to do with money. For many years, the dentist had been partners with another dentist, but they had parted ways and the other dentist had retained most of their shared patients, though he had done so by methods that were certainly unethical, if not illegal. Their dentist was still trying to get on his feet, he said. The rent in this building was steeper than they might think. Plus, he had Holly to think about, and Holly was full-time.

He liked them a lot, though, and he didn't want to break up a set. If they would agree to make a little less than he'd offered in the paper, and if they were okay with getting paid under the table, he thought he could make it work.

They would and they were, and they shook hands with the dentist and went back to Claudia's apartment to call their parents with the good news.

"Let me talk to Kate for a minute," their father said after the congratulations had passed.

Claudia was lying on the kitchen floor while Kate sat on the counter, and she clicked her thumb down on the receiver, then covered the mouthpiece with her palm and slid her thumb back off, listening.

"How's everything?" their father asked.

"Good," said Kate.

"Your sister seems okay?"

"Uh-huh."

"No sign of Dr. Dickweed?"

"Huh?"

"The professor."

"Oh," Kate said, "no," and Claudia held the phone away from her head as she laughed into the floor.

Kate's father sighed. "So it's still completely over?"

Claudia rolled onto her back, and her hair spilled on the linoleum like a puddle of black ink around her head. She smiled up at Kate, then stuck out her tongue.

"Completely," Kate said.

At their dentist's office, people called to schedule or cancel appointments, and Claudia and Kate would add or remove their names from the appointment book. When patients arrived, Kate and Claudia gave them forms to fill out, then collected the forms and ushered the patients to an examination room. People came back out on wobbly knees, their eyes glassy, their cheeks packed with cotton. Claudia and Kate would collect their money, and if the patients were children, let them choose a treasure from the treasure chest—which was really just a beer cooler painted black and filled with small, crappy toys.

Holly, the dental hygienist, was thirty-four and had moved here from Cincinnati with her husband—not her current husband, but the one before, a real mistake, she told Claudia and Kate, but an understandable one given she'd been so young when she married him, eighteen if they could believe it, and pregnant too, but just barely. Had Claudia and Kate ever been to Cincinnati?

They told her they had not, and she said they shouldn't bother. It was a crap-hole.

Holly had stringy hair and a high, squeaky voice. When Holly married her first husband, she told them, she weighed ninety-three pounds. Ninety-three pounds! Of course, she'd been much, much, much too thin back then. *Dangerously* thin, really. Everyone thought she looked prettier now. More like a woman.

Claudia and Kate hated Holly.

"Her fucking voice!" Claudia would wail as they drove home at night. "It makes me want to drive a pair of scissors through my temple."

The more they disliked Holly, the friendlier Holly became with them. She said she hoped she hadn't given them the wrong idea by telling them about her first marriage. She wanted them to know that she'd been happily married to her second husband for nearly twelve years, had given him three healthy children of his own, and also, she was Mormon now.

"She's lying," Claudia told Kate later.

"About being Mormon?" Kate asked.

"About being happy."

There were often long gaps of time between phone calls or appointments, and then Claudia and Kate would take turns making runs to the vending machines on the third floor, bringing back sodas and chocolate bars and little bags of gummi bears. They sat on the counter and painted their fingernails with Wite-Out, eating candy and planning what Kate would tell Claudia's psychologist the next time they met.

Some afternoons, Holly lingered around their counter, nibbling at their candy and asking Claudia and Kate questions about their lives, then telling them about her own before they had a chance to answer.

"Are you virgins?" she asked, and Claudia snorted while Kate tried to look busy organizing that morning's charts—there were only two, and she stacked one on top of the other, then switched the top one to the bottom, then switched them again.

Holly had lost her virginity when she was thirteen to a boy who was seventeen and working at her stepfather's auto shop. They'd done it in the backseat of a 1977 Crown Vic that had been brought into the shop for faulty steering, and afterward, the boy had bought Holly a root beer from the vending machine. When she thought about it now, Holly said, it made her kind of sad. But she tried to remind herself that she'd had low self-esteem back then, and that it was Cincinnati.

At the office, their dentist often bought them lunch and let them go home early, and though he had given up cigarettes several years ago, he let them use his key to the roof when they took smoke breaks, which, he told them, could get him in a lot of trouble if anyone found out. During one of their smoke breaks on the roof, Holly told Claudia and Kate that their dentist had been treated very poorly by his former business partner when something private was discovered about his personal life. But their dentist had handled the situation with dignity and grace. "He could have made a fuss," Holly told them. "He could have fought for his rights. But he walked away, left like a gentleman."

"Why?" Claudia asked, and Holly's gaze drifted over the parking lot below, across the small, silver roofs of the doctors' sports cars and luxury sedans, the canvas tops of convertibles.

Things hadn't been easy for Holly either, she said. She'd worked in that office for a long time, been friends with the other women who worked there. Thought she'd been friends with them, anyway.

"You're not friends now?" Kate asked, and Holly stubbed her cigarette out with the toe of her shoe.

Sometimes friendships were difficult in offices, Holly said. "You know how women can be," she told Kate, and her eyes darted sideways at Claudia. "Mean."

Claudia stared down at Holly's cigarette butt and her mouth crept back into a slanted half-smile. "I didn't know Mormons were allowed to smoke."

That afternoon, Claudia and Kate paused beside Holly's minivan as they crossed the parking lot to their car. The van was rusty and covered with dents and scratches and drawings her children had made in the dirt with their fingers. Claudia glanced around the parking lot to see that she and Kate were alone, then made a gash along the driver's door with her car key.

Kate clamped her hands over her mouth to silence the cry

she felt rising inside. The mark was five or six inches long—sizable, significant, not an accident. But it blended in with the existing wounds of the car, and there was a good chance Holly, or anyone else, wouldn't notice.

Still, Kate felt the panic rolling across her like waves, the unsteadiness of what Claudia had just done, the door she had opened. And when nothing happened, no sirens went off and no men in uniforms came to drag them away, the panic brightened into a giddiness that Kate felt rushing through her joints like champagne bubbles.

"Why?" she asked, and Claudia shrugged.

"We hate her."

Claudia's psychologist thought they needed to work on impulse control. Five times a day, they were supposed to tell themselves no. They were supposed to say no to things they really wanted. They were supposed to say no and mean it.

"That's stupid," Claudia said. "I don't want to."

Their dentist had given them permission to come in late on Thursdays so that Kate could meet with Claudia's psychologist, though he thought that he had given them permission to come in late so that they could tutor slow readers at the YMCA. This week, Kate had told Claudia's psychologist about gashing Holly's van in the parking lot. She also told Claudia's psychologist about driving by their dentist's house at night, because she and Claudia had done this several times.

Claudia wanted to get a look at his family, so they'd found his house—they were pretty sure it was his house—but they couldn't see inside. At first, Kate had wondered if this might not be a good idea, but Claudia assured her that it was only natural to be curious about the personal lives of their coworkers, and Kate really did want to see where their dentist lived.

The neighborhood was nice enough, but the gutters on their dentist's house were swollen and sagging with rotting leaves, and the yard was brown and weedy. "Guess things are a little slow-going at the new practice," Claudia said.

From Holly they'd learned that their dentist had a wife and three children, though he worked very hard and didn't get to spend much time with them.

"He doesn't wear a ring," Claudia said.

"Lots of men don't wear rings," Kate said—their father didn't wear a ring.

"Does your husband wear a ring?" Claudia asked Holly, who blinked at the floor, then said that he did. "You see?" Claudia told Kate. "Holly's husband wears a ring and our dentist doesn't. He hates his wife."

After her session with Claudia's psychologist, Kate peeled the fake bandage off her hand while she explained to Claudia: It was important for their development as human beings to tell themselves no. No damage to property. No candy for breakfast. No drive-bys. Five times a day: No, no, no, no, no.

Claudia was holding an unlit cigarette in one hand, and when she reached for a lighter with the other, Kate pointed back and forth between them. "No."

Claudia paused for a moment, then pointed back and forth between herself and Kate. "Um . . . *No*," she said and lit her cigarette.

The day their dentist's wife came into the office with his children, Claudia rushed around the desk to get a look at them.

"I've heard so much about you," she gasped without thinking, and their dentist's wife looked alarmed.

"You have?"

Claudia's face went slack for a moment and then she smiled, recovering. "Well," she said, "I've heard that you're lovely." Then she reached out as if offering to take their coats, though it was summer so they had none.

Their dentist's wife *was* lovely, and Kate could tell by Claudia's sudden loss of composure that she'd not been expecting this. Her hair was smooth, her clothes chic and simple, and she stood with her purse in her hands, asking Claudia and Kate polite questions about their hometown while she waited for her husband.

The children—two scarecrow girls and a boy with buck teeth—knelt around the cooler while their mother waited, sinking their fingers into the heaps of rubber rings and plastic charms, letting the toy whistles and pencil erasers spill over their hands. After a few moments, their mother whispered that the toys were for patients, and the children closed the lid gently and backed away with their eyes on the carpet.

When the dentist finally came out to speak to his wife, the two went back into his office and closed the door. Claudia looked after them for a moment like a frantic dog, then turned her attention to their children.

"What grade are you in?"

"Fourth," the oldest girl answered after a moment.

"What's your teacher's name?"

"Miss B."

"Miss *Bee*?"

"Miss *B*," the girl said and wrote the letter in the air with her index finger. "It's short for something."

"Is she fat?" Claudia asked, and the children looked at one another, surprised. "My fourth-grade teacher was fat," Claudia said. "She had these fat feet that pudged out over her pumps, and she used to steal the desserts out of our lunch boxes while we were at recess."

The children stared up at her, their eyes wide, their lips parted in wonder. "I swear to God," Claudia told them. "I didn't get a Little Debbie or a Hostess for a whole year." Then she reached behind the counter for their stash of vending machine candy. "Want some gummi bears?" she asked, and their eyes floated dreamily across her face, their mouths widening into lovesick smiles. "My kids think you're an angel," their dentist told Claudia after they'd gone, and Claudia held her hands up as though she had no explanation.

"Kids think I'm swell."

Later on the roof, Claudia leaned against the ledge, gazing out over the parking lot as she smoked. "I can't believe she's so pretty," she said.

"I know," said Kate, although she had not spent much time anticipating the appearance of their dentist's wife and therefore had no real expectations.

"I mean, she's really pretty," Claudia went on.

"She is," said Kate, for she was.

"So much prettier than Holly."

"*So* much," Kate agreed, then, "So?"

Claudia turned and smiled as though Kate was about to say something obvious and amusing. When Kate said nothing, Claudia's face cleared and she blinked.

"What?" Kate asked.

Claudia turned and Kate felt, suddenly, that they were standing a great distance apart. But then Claudia shook her head, pulling Kate close to rest her chin on Kate's shoulder.

"You can pick what we watch tonight," Claudia yawned, for this was their only point of consistent disagreement: Kate had grown bored with plantations. There was too much sobbing, too much violence, too much love of land and country. Kate wanted to spend more time with the Victorians. She loved all the secrets and guilt and groping in gardens.

A few days later, Claudia fell on the apartment stairs and chipped her front tooth. The chip was large and obvious and made her look homely and slightly stupid. She lay facedown on her bed, weeping. Now that she knew what it was like to have a chipped tooth, Claudia said, she couldn't believe she'd wanted to kill herself over love.

When Kate suggested that they might find the chip and glue it back in, Claudia sat up and slapped her across the face. The slap was not hard, but Kate began to cry, and Claudia got up and locked herself in the bathroom.

The next morning, Claudia would not speak to Kate. As soon as they arrived at work, she rushed into their dentist's office and closed the door behind her. When they came back out, her eyes were wet from crying and their dentist had his arm around her. He led her into the light, then cupped her chin in his hand and tilted her face up, squinting into her mouth. "Piece of cake," he said.

He would sand the tooth until the chip disappeared, then sand the tooth beside it so they matched.

Claudia gaped at him. Couldn't he just cap it?

That would be expensive, he said. And this would be free. Besides, he added, Claudia's front teeth were kind of long to begin with. They made her look a little horsey.

Kate reached for her front teeth with her tongue, trying

to measure their length as she followed her sister and their dentist to one of the examination rooms.

"This will feel a little funny," their dentist said to Claudia, "and it will smell bad." Then there was a sound like a cement grinder, and the room filled with a hot stink that made Kate gag into the back of her wrist.

When it was over, their dentist held up a mirror and Claudia squealed, then leaped up to kiss him. "Oh my God!" she gasped. "I'm so much prettier than I was before!"

After work, Claudia drove Kate home and dropped her off. "Where are you going?" Kate asked, but Claudia wouldn't say.

When their father called that night, Kate told him that Claudia was at a movie. For a moment, there was silence. "Kate," he said evenly.

"I don't know where she is," Kate said.

Claudia came back to the apartment at 11:30, and Kate gave her the message to call home. She stared for a moment, then crossed to the phone and dialed. Her voice was bright and friendly as she explained to their father that she'd been hired to babysit their dentist's kids in the evenings and to help his wife around the house. Their father must have approved of this because Claudia thanked him and said that she was really trying to participate and make connections. Then she asked how his day had been.

After she hung up the phone, Claudia crossed to her bedroom and closed the door without so much as glancing in Kate's direction.

Without Claudia to tell her what to say, Kate was unsure how to proceed with Claudia's psychologist. She no longer knew where Claudia went or what she did, and so she couldn't pass the information along. This was frustrating for both of them. "How has your week been?" Claudia's psychologist asked, and Kate said, "I don't know."

Throughout the workday, Claudia found ways to be wherever Kate was not. If Kate was in the reception area, Claudia disappeared into the filing closet. When Kate went up to the roof to have a cigarette, Claudia went down to the parking lot. Kate offered Claudia a bag of gummi bears, and Claudia held one hand to her stomach as though the very sight of the packaging made her ill. "I'm trying to *not* commit suicide, remember?"

At night, Kate would lie awake in her bed, waiting for the sound of Claudia's key in the door and thinking about the house her father had promised her, the house Claudia had said they could live in together. Now Kate pictured a small brick house amid a sea of small brick houses, a place where she would wander from empty room to empty room, a grown-up version of herself living out a grown-up version of her life.

The week before Kate's last meeting with Claudia's psychologist, Claudia took the car for lunch and didn't come back for three hours. When Kate asked where she had been, Claudia glided off to the filing room. "I don't have to tell you everything I do, Kate," she said as she passed. "You're not my fucking diary."

At the end of the day they sat with their purses on their laps, not looking at each other, while they waited for their dentist to finish with his last patient so that they could collect the bill and go home.

The patient was a round little boy who was having four cavities filled. When he came out, his cheeks were flushed and his eyes were soaked and swollen from crying. He held

an ice pack to his jaw and walked with tiny, fragile steps. Kate
led him to the treasure chest and he knelt before it like it was
an altar, waiting for her to open it and reveal all the glorious
bounty within. After she did, he peered inside, then looked
up at her. "These toys suck," he said.

The boy's mother was still in the waiting room, and Claudia leaned forward over the counter and lowered her voice.
"Your face sucks," she whispered, and the boy's lips parted,
novocaine-slack with shock, before he started to cry.

Kate stood to the side, watching. The little boy's mother
had been curt and superior when she'd checked him in, and
Kate felt good for a moment knowing that her sister had hurt
his feelings. It was almost like she'd done it herself.

That night, Claudia dropped Kate off at the apartment,
then went to babysit their dentist's children. She came home
late and went to bed without speaking to Kate. A few nights
later, she didn't come home at all.

Without Claudia and her car, Kate couldn't get to work, so
she didn't go. She wandered around Claudia's apartment,
looking through Claudia's closet and dresser drawers, trying
on her clothes, reading her journals and old school papers.
She found some pictures of Claudia naked and some poems
someone had written about Claudia and an engagement ring
with a note saying that Claudia should keep the ring anyway
and think of him sometimes, love always, Paul.

When, at last, Kate's father called, she thought he would
come straightaway, would figure out where Claudia was and
what she was doing, then would make her stop at once and
come home. But when Kate answered the phone, her father
didn't ask about Claudia. He was crying, and a long moment

passed before he spoke—he and her mother had decided it would be best for everyone if he moved into the city for a while.

Kate had probably seen this coming, her father said, and Kate told him that she had, not because she had at all seen it coming, but because—now that she thought about it—she saw that she should have.

The day of her last meeting with Claudia's psychologist, Kate walked to the college with the sunlight spilling between the leaves. If Claudia did not come back, maybe Kate could just stay here, could live in Claudia's apartment and attend Claudia's college. It would be easy enough to say that Kate was the sister who went missing, to let it be Kate's life that went unfinished.

But during their final session, Claudia's psychologist told Kate that though it had been a pleasure getting to know her, it was her opinion that Claudia should not enroll in fall classes. Then she told Kate that she was, at her heart, a very gentle person, and that she shouldn't be ashamed of that.

A few days later there was no food left in Claudia's apartment, so Kate quit eating. She drank water and Lipton tea and returned to Claudia's closet hourly to check the increasing ease with which she slid into Claudia's clothing. The phone rang several times, then Kate unplugged it. She stopped looking out the window. She stopped listening for Claudia's footsteps outside. She closed the curtains and counted her ribs and thought about those fallen belles and mad wives of gentlemen, the women left alone in decomposing mansions and drafty attics, the ones who, in the end, always set fire to everything.

When, at last, a knock came at the door, Kate answered with her legs wobbly and her thoughts loose in her head. This would be her mother, probably, here to collect her, here to fall to pieces when she realized Claudia was missing, had been missing for, what was it now, eleven days? Or her father, who would shout horrible things, things Kate deserved to have shouted at her, for she had called no one, told no one, that Claudia was missing, and what if something terrible had happened, what if Claudia was dead? Until this moment the thought had not actually occurred to her: What if Claudia was dead?

Kate opened the door, and their dentist's lovely wife stood on the doorstep twisting her lovely hands. She'd been crying and her hair was wet, which made Kate think that it was raining, though it wasn't. For a moment, Kate thought this must be a dream, one of those mundane, immediately forgotten scenes in which some slight acquaintance suddenly takes the main stage, but then their dentist's wife told Kate that it was over with their dentist, and her perfume passed across the threshold like a lilac-scented breeze.

She was beautiful in the way that women in magazines are beautiful, sloped and elegant. Kate's sister had stolen the husband of a beautiful woman—why else would she be here?—and now, in Claudia's absence, Kate would have to pay.

Inside the apartment, the light was dim and their dentist's wife perched on the edge of Claudia's futon, squinting at Claudia's bong in a way that made Kate wonder if she'd ever seen one before. Kate asked if she wanted some and she shook her head, then pointed at the pack of cigarettes beside it. She'd take one of those, though.

Kate gave her a cigarette and watched her light it, then sit and smoke in silence.

She'd made a lot of mistakes in her life, their dentist's wife said finally. She hadn't meant to, but she had. She'd once cheated on their dentist with an old boyfriend. But she'd done this only once, and she'd felt like shit every single second of every single day ever since. You could live with a secret for so long, she told Kate, that the secret became the only thing you knew was true about yourself.

Kate should have put together what was happening. But a moment later their dentist's wife was thanking her for her courage and her honesty, her strength of character, her sense of decency. And though Kate could not think of a single reason for their dentist's wife to thank her for anything, she was momentarily so drunk on the praise and gratitude that she could not be bothered to question its ill fit. And it wasn't until their dentist's wife took both of Kate's hands in hers and said, "If you hadn't told me what he was up to with Holly, I don't know how many more years I would have gone without knowing," that Kate realized she'd been taken for Claudia.

Claudia left with her professor. He'd had a change of heart over the summer. Decided he couldn't live without her after all. Had been a fool. Et cetera.

Years later, Claudia would write Kate a letter, trying to explain. She'd been young and vulnerable, in terrible pain. She'd never meant to put Kate in the middle of such a mess or to leave her to handle that incident with their mother and the sleeping pills shortly after. Claudia was so very sorry, she wrote in that letter, to have learned about Kate's recent troubles in love. Perhaps in her current situation, Kate might at least imagine how Claudia could have behaved so atrociously that summer.

Along with her letter, Claudia sent a check for fifty dollars with her apologies for missing so many birthdays, and a photo she had cut from a magazine—a portrait of a famous actress in character as the famous photographer she was about to portray on film. Claudia was including the picture, she wrote, because when she'd first seen it, she'd thought it was Kate.

The famous actress did not resemble the famous photographer and neither of them particularly resembled Kate, but the photograph captured the ghost of an expression, and for a queer moment, Kate too thought she had seen herself.

They should try harder to keep in touch, Claudia wrote at the end of her letter. She would like to be better friends. They were sisters, after all.

Kate put the letter away somewhere. But the portrait of the actress-photographer kicked around for a while and was the subject of much conversation. In the year or so before it disappeared into clutter or was tossed in a move, no one who saw the image—not even those who knew Kate very, very well—could pass by without asking, "Is that you?"

Femme

You have known us since childhood. We are Simone or Cat, Rhonda or Nicole. We have cool voices and long eyelashes. We wear too much makeup or not enough. We are your classmate, your coworker, your next-door neighbor. We can tell that you are not like us and we find this attractive. We want to spend time with you. We want to be your friend.

When we invite you to coffee, we talk about books and movies, about places we used to live and men we used to date. It is innocent—*girl* talk. We admire your manners, your clothes, the way you're wearing your hair today. You don't have to feel guarded around us. You can tell us your secrets. Of course we will keep them. You can trust us. You want to trust us.

We are good listeners. We nod knowingly while you speak and make little noises in the backs of our throats, sympathetic encouragement. We want to know more about your family. We watch while you talk, catching the weaknesses in your expression, the moments your eyes dart sideways or your lips quiver. We notice each time your fingers catch on the tablecloth as you talk about your mother, how she is lonely, how she calls you on the phone three times a day and cries from missing you so much. Of course you feel guilty. Who wouldn't? But you can't, we tell you, *can't* allow other people to have so much control over you. Your life belongs to *you,* we say. You have to be your own person. You tell us about your father, how he calls drunk and bellows at you, how he cuts you off, then begs you to forgive him. We say the words you don't allow yourself to say: *jackass, bastard, lunatic.*

You work too hard. You need to take time for yourself. Call in sick. Go on vacation. *Spoil yourself.* If you don't look after your best interests, who will? Don't be afraid to splurge, to let someone else do the work for a change. You've earned a break. Get a manicure, we tell you. Get a facial. Buy the shoes that don't go with anything and the dress you know you'll never wear.

We don't have many friends, but we trust you. We let you get close to us. Your other friends are suspicious, but you are sorry that they don't know us the way you do. They don't see our fragile side, don't know what you know. You can sense our pain, sense that we have been betrayed or wounded, abandoned or misused. We have allowed you access we don't allow everyone. You see us as we *really* are. You are special.

You tell us about your other friends. You feel guilty speaking about them, but you are annoyed, frustrated. You don't always trust their motives. You feel pressured by their demands on you. You're worn out by the effort it takes to be with them, to feign interest in their stream of never-ending problems. You're tired of pretending to like their husbands: the alcoholic, the liar, the loser, the asshole. Every time you answer the phone, someone is crying, someone is raging, someone is begging you to solve their problems.

"I'm just not happy," they say.

"I feel ugly."

"When do things get *easy*?"

"He said he *loved* me."

Your other friends, they are uneasy around us, quiet and nervous. But we know them only as acquaintances. You can talk about them all you like—it isn't betrayal. Everyone has to vent sometimes, we tell you. And we are safe. When you confront your mother, we send you flowers. When you hang up on your father, we bring you cheesecake at work. We make you laugh. No one has ever understood you the way that we do.

We stay quiet when you tell us about your relationship with your husband, about the strangeness between you, the distance. You love him, but when you look at him now, you can't remember what it felt like to fall in love with him. You can't remember who you were when you married him. You live like comfortable strangers. Like characters in a play. You don't know if he feels the same way you do. You are afraid.

Last week, you came home from work and found him sitting naked in an empty bathtub, crying into his knees. You worry that you are not as afraid as you ought to be. You begin sifting through his wallet when he is out of the room, looking for phone numbers you don't recognize. When you do the laundry now, you sniff at the collars of his shirts, searching for hints of another woman's perfume. We stroke your hair when you tell us this. It's all right, we say. Your feelings are just your feelings. You don't have to validate them. *Cry* if you need to cry. You're going through a hard time, that's all. We want to help. We want to *be there* for you.

In grade school, we were the friends who told you to steal that lipstick from the drugstore. It's just a *lipstick*, we told you. They would never miss it. We kept watch for you. And then we kept quiet when you called us, crying, wondering how in the world your mother had found out. In high school, we giggled with you when you confessed your secret crush to us, your Rick or Sam or Alex. Then we shrugged helplessly when he asked us to the winter formal. You have met us a hundred times before. But still, you don't recognize us. Still, you don't see us coming until we have gone.

After you figure out how we are, you say that nothing we do will surprise you. You make excuses for us: difficult childhood, low self-esteem, loneliness. You say that we are a blessing in disguise. A litmus test. You believe that we are unhappy. You feel sorry for us. But these are the things you have to say. You have told us too much. When you speak of us, you have to be kind. You have made us too powerful.

Everything you have, we can take. Everything you want, we can get first. We will watch what you do and we will do it better. We know how to look weak, how to look hurt, how to look harmless. You can't turn on us. You can't send us away. You have let us into your world. We drink with your friends and play poker with your husband. We are familiar with him. We touch his arm in passing. We laugh at his jokes and tease him about his clothing. When we run into you, we kiss your cheek. We call you *love, darling,* or *pet.* We ask about your mother and about your work. But we no longer smile when you walk into a room. We don't always meet your eye when you pass. We are often too preoccupied to notice you at all. We will stop finding time to have coffee. We will forget to return your calls. We will sleep with your husband or not sleep with him. You will never know.

Slowly, we will realize that your life doesn't fit us better than any of the others we have tried on. We know your friends now. They are more interesting than you are. They have stranger frailties, quirkier husbands, uglier secrets. You can't warn them against us. You will try once or twice and then give up. But your friends will learn and eventually we will move out of your sphere altogether. And then you will be free to talk about us, to volley stories about us with your friends, *But did I tell you what she did to me?* You will decide that after everything, we were surprisingly ineffectual. We didn't take anything you couldn't get back. Your friends, your family, your problems, your world, they all belong to you again. And maybe you will forget that there were moments when you wanted us to have them. You will forget the moments when you wanted to give everything away.

You will stop hating us. You will think of us less and less, forget what we looked like, forget the things you told us. And in the end, we will occupy only a fragment of your life: a picture in a yearbook, a certain table at a certain coffee shop, a scratch between your college roommate and your husband's godfather on your Christmas card list. You should feel good about yourself. You weren't conquered, weren't destroyed. Your life belongs to you, just like we always told you it did.

Allegiance

On her first day at the American school, Glynnis's class dissects earthworms. At her old school, the fourth-graders dissected cow eyes that came delivered in a plastic jug. But here, the worms aren't delivered. After lunch, the class has to find their own worms in the mud outside, then rinse them off in the bathroom sinks. Glynnis's new teacher partners her with Leora Faust, a girl with crooked teeth and patchy brown bruises on her knees. Everyone else already has a partner.

That morning, Glynnis's father drove her to the new school on his way to work. Her mother had refused to come along. "American children bring guns to school," she said and kissed Glynnis on the top of the head. "So try not to piss anyone off." Her father grew up in this town, and along the drive he pointed out things he remembered: a tire store that used to be an ice cream shop, a small park that used to be a big park, a bank that has always been a bank but used to have a different name.

Glynnis got to sit at her desk while the rest of the class stood to say the Pledge of Allegiance. She told her teacher that it would be treason for her to say it, that if they found out in England, they could have her head chopped off. Miss Glen cocked her head to one side and said, "Well, we wouldn't want that, would we?" Until Glynnis was paired with Leora Faust, no one else had spoken to her.

Glynnis stands to the side, watching as Leora reads the directions from her science book. At the desk behind hers, a boy uses his knife to lift a sliver of guts from his worm. "Hey, Mary Poppins!" he says and thrusts his knife toward Glynnis.

Two girls with matching Princess Leia buns in their hair laugh as Glynnis darts sideways. "Jer-e-*mi*-ah!" they squeal, and Glynnis tries to smile, tries to take the joke. At her old school, the disturbed children had their own classroom in the basement, and even in there, Glynnis is pretty sure they weren't allowed to hold knives.

It's a mess, this new school, a dirty scab of a place with orange carpet in the hallways and soggy hamburgers at lunch. Because the rain made the playground muddy, the class has to take their shoes off when they come inside and pile them up next to the door. Glynnis has spent the whole day feeling cold and grubby in her socks. In England, they always got to wear their shoes inside.

"Check it out," Jeremiah says to the Princess Leia girls and aims his knife at Leora Faust. As she bends forward over her science book, Jeremiah flicks his knife, springing worm guts onto the back of her head. Leora continues reading, keeping her place with her finger while the guts stick in her hair, dangling like a tiny slick sausage.

Miss Glen is circling through the classroom, answering questions and leaning over to inspect work. When she comes up behind them, Glynnis holds her breath. Someone will have to tell. It isn't like Jeremiah made a nasty face or called Leora a name. There are *dead* parts hanging in her hair. Glynnis is sure the Princess Leia girls will say something. At her old school, it was always girls against boys.

Miss Glen stops and touches her crimson fingernails to one of the girls' perfect braided buns. "Megan R. and Megan C.," she says. "You two always have the prettiest hair." Glynnis waits. This is the time to tell. Miss Glen is on their side.

"My mom does it," one of the Megans says. "Megan C. comes over before school and my mom does us both."

The Megans turn back to their work. Miss Glen is walking past. Glynnis stares down at her desk so that she won't have to see the worm guts, the slick greasy string of them, shivering in Leora's hair. So this is America, then. Nobody is going to do anything.

While Glynnis and her father eat supper that night, her mother sits at the table, smoking cigarettes and drinking red wine from a paper cup. "Aren't you eating?" her father asks.

"I hate the food here," her mother says and waves her cigarette in front of her. "Everything tastes like cheese or chocolate."

"It's just *soup*," says her father.

"It's easy for you," her mother says. "You've been eating so much of this garbage, you stink of it. Both of you." Glynnis puts her spoon down and sniffs at her shoulder. The new house smells like fresh paint and carpet cleaner. The yard smells like wet dirt. But her shoulder smells normal enough.

Glynnis's father smiles and blinks his eyes quickly. "How

about we try to be a little positive? Glynnis?" He raises his eyebrows at her. "Tell us one thing about your new school."

Glynnis opens her mouth to tell them about Jeremiah throwing worm guts into Leora's hair, but before any sound can come out, her father holds up his hand. "No," he says. "Something *good*."

Glynnis stops. Her father is watching, tapping his plastic spoon on the edge of his paper bowl. "I don't know," she says finally.

"Your teacher's pretty," he says, and her mother makes a choking noise. "Don't you think?"

Glynnis hasn't really thought about it, but she supposes Miss Glen is all right. She isn't old or fat or covered with big hairy moles. "Sure," Glynnis says. "She's pretty enough."

She can see the cords in her mother's neck tightening, the skin around her lips pulling thin. "Well," she says to Glynnis's father. "Thank *God-bless-America* for that."

"Taxation without representation. What does that even *mean*?" her mother asks while Glynnis is in the bathtub. Glynnis is trying to explain about the social studies lesson. They love their wars, Americans, love to talk about them and watch filmstrips about them and look at pictures of them in books. Only her first day and already Glynnis knows all about George Washington and the Redcoats and Paul Revere screaming his head off across the countryside. *The British are coming! The British are coming!*

"You'd think they would have gotten over it by now," her mother says. "A slight overcharge for tea and we're still on their list."

"Miss Glen says it was a long time ago," Glynnis tells her

mother. "She says that America saved us in a couple of big wars and so we're all great friends again."

"She sounds like a nincompoop," her mother says and bends over Glynnis, clipping the wet ends of her hair to the top of her head with a barrette. This is their time together, *girl time,* her mother calls it. Her father never bothers them, never knocks or calls or tries to come in. But still, her mother locks the door.

"Did you make any friends?" her mother asks and sits down on the lid of the toilet.

Glynnis scrubs herself hard with the soap, just in case the food smell is still on her. "There was one girl," she says. "We cut up a worm together."

Her mother's face freezes.

"It was for science," Glynnis says. "Miss Glen made us partners."

Her mother closes her eyes and smiles. "Oh," she says. "That doesn't count then. You didn't make a friend." She stands up and peels out of her blue jeans and sweater, dropping them onto the floor. "Scoot up," she says. "I'm getting in."

Glynnis moves forward, pulling her knees to her chest as her mother lowers herself into the water behind her. She rubs Glynnis's back with the heel of her hand. "Was school terrible?" she asks, and Glynnis slides back between her mother's legs, leaning onto her chest.

"They never raise their hands," she says. "Nobody talks to me and the classroom smells like dirty feet."

"It's the same way here," her mother says. She touches her mouth to the top of Glynnis's head. "I miss home."

"So do I," says Glynnis.

"I was *born* there," her mother whispers.

"So was I," says Glynnis.

Her mother touches one wet finger to the curve of Glynnis's ear, tracing the lobe with her fingernail. "What does your teacher look like?"

Glynnis tries to think. "She has black hair and brown eyes," she says. "She paints her fingernails red. And she smiles a lot."

Glynnis can feel the rise and fall of her mother's chest against her shoulder blades. "Can I sleep in your bed tonight?" her mother asks, and Glynnis nods. Her mother circles her wet arms around Glynnis's shoulders. "Nobody loves you as much as I do," she says.

"I know," says Glynnis.

Her mother tightens her arms and dips her head forward so that Glynnis can feel her breath on the back of her ear. "Now you say it to me," her mother whispers.

"No one loves you as much as I do."

The cafeteria doesn't have enough chocolate milk for everyone in line. Because of this, it is a race to be first. Miss Glen tries to make it fair. "Today," she says to the class, "people with the letter *M* in their name may be the first in line." Megan R. and Megan C. clap their hands and run to the door, cramming their feet into matching pink sneakers. Glynnis puts her chin in her hand and waits. Next come people with *B*, then *H*. Most of the class is in line and Glynnis feels the sadness inside her like a bag of wet sand. She doesn't even like chocolate milk.

When Miss Glen calls *L*, Glynnis slides out of her desk and follows Leora Faust to the back of the line. Miss Glen starts to lead the class into the hallway, and Glynnis hurries to get her laces tied.

"My shoe's gone!" Leora yells, and Miss Glen stops. "Somebody stole my shoe!"

Miss Glen walks to the back of the line, her bright mouth puckered like a prune. "Leora," she says, and she sounds tired. "No one *stole* your shoe. Let's hurry now so that we don't make everyone late for lunch."

Leora looks like she is about to cry. Everyone is watching. Crying is the absolute wrong thing to do. "I can't find my shoe," Leora says, and her voice is small and squeaky.

Miss Glen closes her eyes and rubs her forehead with her fingers. "Let's all look for Leora's shoe," she says and sighs at the ceiling.

When Jeremiah pulls the shoe out of the trash can, he swings it at Leora by its laces. "Somebody must have thought it was garbage," he says.

On the way to the lunchroom, the hallway echoes with shouts of "Leora-shoe-germs! No touch-backs!" One by one, the shoe germs pass down the line. Glynnis walks behind Leora, who hasn't taken the time to put her shoes all the way on and clip-clops down the hallway with her heels bunched out over the backs. When the germs pass to Leora, they stop. She does not turn around to pass her own germs to Glynnis.

In the cafeteria, Glynnis eats lunch by herself. At the table beside hers, Megan R. is passing out pink envelopes with stickers on them. "It's a slumber party," she tells the girls at her table. "My mom is buying mud masks and cucumbers so we can do facials."

"Your birthday parties are always the best, Megan," says one of the girls.

"I know," says Megan R. "But it's going to be expensive and my mom won't let me have as many people this year. We have to keep it a secret." The rest of the girls smile, and

Megan R. lowers her voice. "I don't want people to have their *feelings* hurt."

Parents are to blame for this. At some point in the early party-planning, parents said how many people got to come, how many friends your life had room for. Sometime, weeks before Glynnis even existed at this school, Megan R.'s mother had said a number. A list was made. Glynnis sits alone at her table, sipping her plain white milk and waiting for the bell to ring so that she can throw her food away and go back to the classroom.

After school, Glynnis sits cross-legged on her bed while her mother stands naked in front of the closet. At the new house, all the closet doors are made of mirrors, and this is what her mother does now while her father is at work—look at herself naked.

"There's one girl at school that everybody's mean to," Glynnis tells her mother. "Even the teacher."

Her mother is standing sideways in front of the mirror, pulling the skin on her stomach smooth, then letting it pooch again. "It's like that sometimes," she says. "For some people, it's like that." This is something that Glynnis appreciates about her mother, the way she doesn't pretend like she can fix things.

"Why?" Glynnis asks, and her mother shrugs.

"Some people just make it too easy," she says. "They make it too easy for people to be mean."

Glynnis thinks about this. At her old school there was a girl who said loud, screechy prayers before every meal and every exam, always *Jesus* this and *Jesus* that. But nobody ever threw her shoes in the bin. Nobody ever passed her germs around. "But why doesn't she have any friends?" Glynnis asks, and her mother turns to look at her.

"*I* don't have any friends," she says.

"At home you do," Glynnis says. "You have lots."

"No." Her mother crosses her arms over her breasts, pressing them flat against her body. "I don't."

Glynnis uses her fingernail to scrape a piece of dried mud off the bottom of her shoe. "What about Judy?" she asks and flicks the clump of mud off the bedspread. "What about Rachel and Linda and Katie Bell from across the street? They're all your friends."

"Not anymore," her mother says. "I don't have any friends anymore."

The girls, that's what her mother called them. They had grown up together, had gone to the same schools, listened to the same music, told the same stories about the same people. When Glynnis came home in the afternoons she would find them on the back porch, smoking cigarettes and sipping cocktails out of fancy glasses. *"Girls,"* they whispered to one another when they had something important to say. Glynnis would sit on her mother's lap and take tiny sips from her frosted glass while they talked about old boyfriends and first kisses, women they'd known who had gotten fat or poor or divorced. They finished one another's sentences, her mother's friends, clipping their stories together, filling in one another's missing details, telling jokes in unison, screaming with laughter at the mention of a name, a place, a word that meant nothing to Glynnis.

Her mother's friends called her father *the American,* and when he came home from work they would take turns dancing with him around the kitchen table. "You're lucky," they told him while the radio played in the background. "American women are loud and fat. They chew with their mouths open." He wagged his finger at them while Glynnis and her mother laughed into their hands. "Don't you ever let him steal you away," they said to Glynnis's mother, and she promised that she wouldn't.

"How come they're not your friends anymore?" Glynnis asks. "Is it because we moved?"

Her mother is staring at her reflection, tracing the tips of her fingers along her lips, pressing them into the hollows beneath her eyes. "Ask your father," she says, and Glynnis sits up straight.

"Why did we come here?" she asks.

Her mother looks down at the carpeting, pushing the knobs of her knees together as she lifts up onto her toes. "He lied," she says. "He lied to me."

Glynnis thinks about this. One little lie doesn't seem like such an important thing. If that's the only reason, then maybe they don't have to stay here. They're not even unpacked yet. "Maybe he's sorry," Glynnis says and climbs to her knees. "*Really* sorry, I mean. Like that time I spilled grape juice on the carpet and blamed it on the lady who used to clean our house? Maybe it's like that!"

"It isn't," her mother says. "It isn't at all like that." She narrows her eyes at Glynnis in the mirror. "And you can just stop bouncing up and down because we aren't going back."

Glynnis sinks back onto her heels and her mother lifts her breasts, pinching the nipples between her fingers. "Do you think I'm ugly?" she asks.

"No," Glynnis says, and her mother sighs.

"You have to say that," she says. "You look just like me."

For supper, her mother gives them cheese macaroni on paper plates, then sits at the table smoking a cigarette and drinking from her paper cup. Her father takes a big bite of macaroni and then gives them the thumbs-up sign. "Super!" he says, and her mother makes a hissing noise in the back of her throat. "Not eating?" he asks, and when her mother doesn't answer, he claps his hands and rubs them together. "Well," he says, smiling. "Let's hear something good about school, Glynnis."

Glynnis looks at her mother to see if she has to answer, but her mother's head is tilted backward, blowing smoke rings at the ceiling. "The coolest girls are Megan R. and Megan C.," she says. "They wear matching hair and pink shoes and everybody wants to be friends with them."

"That's nice," her father says.

"It's Megan R.'s birthday on Friday and she's having a slumber party. Only the best girls get to go."

Her mother's head snaps up. "A slumber party!" she says and shimmies her shoulders over the table. "I *loved* slumber parties. We used to laugh until we threw up!"

"Charming," her father says, but her mother ignores him.

"We used to put a girl's fingers in warm water while she was sleeping so that she would wet herself." Her mother dips her head forward, laughing into her chest. "Then when she woke up, we'd push her outside and lock the door so that she'd have to ring the bell and walk through the house in front of everyone!"

"You did that to your friends?" Glynnis asks, and her mother cocks her head.

"Of course not," she says. "Well, not to the *good* ones, anyway."

"Why would you do that to anyone?" Glynnis asks, and her mother rolls her eyes.

"For *fun*," she says.

"It doesn't *sound* like fun," Glynnis says, and her father coughs into his shoulder.

"Maybe not to *you*," her mother says. "You're such a stick."

"I'm not invited to go anyway," Glynnis says, and her father looks up.

"Why not?" he asks.

Glynnis blinks at her plate of macaroni. "I'm new."

Her father reaches across the table and puts his hand on top of hers. "You won't be new for long," he says and squeezes her fingers. Glynnis feels a knot pressing into the back of her throat. She wants to close her eyes and lean her head forward onto the back of her father's wrist.

"You were supposed to be a Megan," her mother says, and Glynnis looks up at her. "Up until the very last second. But your father changed his mind."

"What?" Glynnis asks.

"Oh," he says. "Yeah. It reminded me of breakfast. Eggs and bagels or something. I don't know. I liked Glynnis." He smiles at her across the table. "Aren't you lucky to be one of a kind?"

Her mother watches as Glynnis slides her hand away from her father and drops it into her lap.

After her bath that night, Glynnis sits on her bed while her mother plays with the radio, turning through static until she finds a station with bright, bouncy music. "Want me to paint your fingernails?" she asks, and Glynnis shakes her head. Her insides are still jumping at the near miss of her own stupid name.

"I'm really tired," Glynnis says, but her mother shakes the little bottle in front of her.

"Oh, come on," she says. "It'll make you pretty."

At lunch the next day, Miss Glen announces that people with pink fingernails can be first in line, then winks one almond-shaped eye at Glynnis. There is groaning. Both of the Megans have normal, naked fingernails.

While Glynnis is waiting to get her tray, she hears a rustling behind her and turns to see the Megans leaning out of line. "New Girl," Megan R. whispers and waves to get her attention. "Get us a chocolate milk." She thrusts her hand forward and Glynnis looks down at the money.

Nothing good can come of this. If Glynnis takes the money, the Megans will think she is weak, willing to give something for nothing. If she doesn't, they will hate her forever. The Megans narrow their eyes and the rest of the class watches. This is the choice: enemy or servant. Glynnis doesn't know which is worse.

When Leora Faust steps out of line, her eyes are wide and serious. "It's against the rules," she says to Glynnis. "It's cheating and it's against the rules."

"M-Y-O-B," says Megan C., and Leora touches Glynnis on the arm.

"You're not supposed to, Glynnis. Miss Glen might call your mom and then you'll get in trouble." Leora's fingers feel smooth and cold in the crook of Glynnis's elbow, and for a second she wants to put her hand on Leora's bony little shoulder. She wants to tell her not to worry, that everything is going to be fine.

But the Megans turn to each other, speaking with the silent language of their eyes. It is something Glynnis has seen her mother do with her friends, a lengthening of the neck, a raised eyebrow, a slow curl at one side of the mouth. In a moment it will be too late. She has to do something.

"Don't touch me," Glynnis says and yanks her arm away. "*I* don't want your stinky germs."

Leora's breath comes out in one hot gasp. "I'll tell," she says, but her voice is small, buried somewhere deep inside her chest. "I'll tell Miss Glen on all of you."

Megan R. steps forward, resting her hand on one cocked hip. "Then we'll all say you're lying," she says. Leora looks down at her scruffy brown shoes, and Glynnis snatches the money from Megan R. A second, maybe less, and they are all back in line.

"I was almost a Megan," Glynnis says when they sit down at her table. She passes them each a chocolate milk, and Megan C. looks at her doubtfully.

"Almost?" she asks.

"It's my mother's favorite name in the world," Glynnis tells them. "But my father changed it at the last second."

"Why didn't your mom stop him?" Megan R. asks. "If that's what she wanted to name you?"

Glynnis thinks about this. "He lied," she says after a moment. "He changed it without telling her and she didn't find out until after."

"That sucks," says Megan R., but she is looking over the top of Glynnis's head, waving to get the attention of the girls who usually sit at her table.

"She's still ripped up about it," Glynnis says. "My mother only calls me *Megan*."

"We have one too many people," Megan R. says, counting chairs around the table. "We'll have to squeeze."

The table fills in around them and Glynnis sits with her elbows pinched to her sides while the other girls talk about the slumber party. "My dad's going to make oysters Rockefeller," Megan R. says. "They're my favorite."

"Oysters?" Glynnis asks, and Megan straightens.

"Have you ever *had* them?" she asks, and Glynnis blushes.

"My dad doesn't cook," she says, and Megan smiles at the rest of the table.

"Well," she says. "You don't know what you're missing."

Glynnis pokes at her lunch. The gravy on her chicken-fried steak is brown and clumpy and she scrapes it to the edge of her tray while the other girls plan prank phone calls and talk about what movies Megan R. should ask her mother to rent for the party.

"At my old school, we used to put a girl's hand in warm water and make her wet herself at slumber parties," Glynnis says, and the rest of the girls look at her.

"Wet herself?" Megan C. asks. "Like, pee her pants?"

Glynnis nods. "We waited for someone to fall asleep and then after we made her wet, er, pee her pants, we'd lock her outside." For one glorious moment, the Megans look at Glynnis and she can feel the doors of her future swing wide open. She will buy pink tennis shoes. She will wear her hair in fancy braids. She will be the Megan with interesting stories—the *continental* Megan.

But even as Glynnis is imagining the three-way phone calls and notes passed in class, the Megans turn toward each other. They touch fingers. Glynnis can feel her lungs empty like two shriveled balloons. It doesn't matter how many stories she has, how many cafeteria rules she breaks. She could eat lunch at this table every day for the rest of her life, go to every party, share in every conversation. Still, she won't ever know them as well as they know each other.

"We have to do that," Megan R. whispers. "Who could we do that to?"

"The water has to be really warm," Glynnis says. "Or else it won't work."

"Leora," Megan C. says. "We should do that to Leora."

Glynnis moves her food around on her tray while the rest of the girls discuss the best way to convince Megan's mom to let her invite an extra person. They will say Leora helped with a social studies project. It might work. Megan R. stands up and crosses the cafeteria to the table where Leora is sitting alone.

Glynnis cannot watch. Leora Faust is small and strange-looking with greasy hair and dirty fingernails. But she has never done anything to Glynnis. Leora can't know the way the world has been planning against her. Glynnis's mother, Megan R.'s mother, they all had a part. Strangers bumped into each other's lives, moved things around without credit or knowledge or blame. One day, Glynnis and her mother had seen her father sitting in the window of a restaurant, sharing a soda with Katie Bell from across the street. And then they'd moved. Snip, snip, snip. The old world fell away and Glynnis was left in this new one. Megan R. was wrong when she said that Glynnis didn't know what she was missing. The whole wide world was just a big pile of strangers, thinking all the time about everything they were missing.

Glynnis's father says that she cannot eat Pop-Tarts for dinner. He peels back the bread from his cheese sandwich and shakes the salt and pepper shakers over the square of yellow cheese. "I've been working all day," he says to her mother. "You could at least unpack some boxes. You could at least *heat something up*."

Her mother doesn't answer. She holds her paper cup against her chest and sways her hips around the kitchen counter, like she is listening to music. Glynnis sits down at the table and uses her teeth to tear open the foil wrapper of her Pop-Tart. Her father looks at her. "I said no," he says. "Not for dinner, Glynnis."

Glynnis looks at her mother, waiting to be told what to do. Her mother glances at the Pop-Tart and then at Glynnis's father. She yawns and clutches her paper cup in both hands as she twirls around the counter and sways quietly out of the room. When Glynnis looks back at her father, he is watching her hard, his mouth small and tight in the corners. Glynnis keeps her eyes on his as she folds back the foil wrapper. He shakes his head, a warning, and Glynnis stares straight at him. Very slowly, she fills her mouth with Pop-Tart and makes her face big with chewing.

When her father stands up, Glynnis is afraid he is going to hit her. He raises his hand and the Pop-Tart turns to concrete inside her mouth, grit and dirt and gravel. But her father doesn't hit her. Instead, he hits the table. He slams the flat of his hand down hard so that the table shakes over Glynnis's legs and the salt and pepper shakers tip sideways, spilling across the wood. "God *damn* it!" he yells.

The words stay in the room even when the sound has stopped. The walls hold them there like a cold, creeping fog. Glynnis stares down at all the salt and pepper loose across the table. She sits in her chair long after her father has left the kitchen, using the ridge of her fingernail to separate the salt and pepper into little piles, salts with salts, peppers with peppers, so they will be with their friends. So they won't be afraid.

"Friday Flip-Up Day!" Jeremiah screams on the playground before school starts. Leora Faust is wearing a skirt with big cartoon frogs on it and the boys chase her around the tire swing, catching the hem of her skirt in their fingers and lifting it over her white underpants.

"Stop it!" she screams, spinning in circles and swatting their hands away like bees. "Leave me alone!"

Jeremiah laughs. "You *know* what Friday is," he tells her. "You shouldn't have worn a skirt."

Leora breaks away, sprinting across the muddy grass to the classroom. Glynnis leans back against the brick wall with the Megans, tugging at her corduroy pants and thanking God that all her skirts are still packed in boxes somewhere.

"Leora's mom said she could come to my party," Megan R. says when the bell rings. "You're so cool for thinking of that warm-water thing. I really wish I could invite you too."

Glynnis follows them into the classroom. "I'm sure your party will be really fun," she says politely. But her head is loose and swimmy on the stem of her neck, her limbs slow and heavy. Glynnis sits through the morning with her head propped on both hands. Her stomach feels like a cold, wet rag and she pushes her fist into it, trying to make it believe she isn't hungry. Glynnis's mother had been asleep by the time she finished with the salt and pepper. She climbed into bed without a bath and pressed her body against her mother's. She had stayed awake all night, listening to the sounds of her stomach sloshing and to the slow, wheezy snorts of her father's breathing coming from the big bedroom where he slept alone.

At recess, Glynnis begins to follow the Megans, but Miss Glen calls her back. "You're looking a little scruffy today," she says. Glynnis looks down to make sure that her blouse is clean, that she's put her shoes on the right feet. "Would you like me to fix your hair for you?" Miss Glen asks, and Glynnis runs her fingers over the back of her head. Her mother was still asleep when Glynnis left for school, and she had tried to put her own hair in a French braid. She worked until her fingers ached, but it had come out wrong, crooked and lumpy.

Glynnis stands perfectly still while Miss Glen uses her fingers to comb out her hair. "So," she says as she divides Glynnis's hair into sections. "It must be hard to be so far from home."

"I suppose so," Glynnis says. She doesn't want to think about England or her old school or the house she used to live in. What's the point? She can't go back.

"Of course, *this* is your home too," Miss Glen says.

Glynnis is quiet. It would be rude to argue with her teacher.

"Your father's American?" Miss Glen asks. Glynnis can feel Miss Glen's hands tugging on her hair as she nods. "So you are too. You have *dual citizenship*. Do you know what that means?" When Glynnis doesn't answer, Miss Glen sighs. "It means you're very special," she says. "You have *two* countries. Everyone else at this school only has one. I think we can all learn *a lot* from each other."

Glynnis is facing the bulletin board, where Miss Glen has taped up a construction-paper version of Betsy Ross's flag. "What if there's a war?" she asks, and the words feel loose and clunky inside her mouth. "Like before?"

Miss Glen snaps the rubber band around the end of Glynnis's braid. "You don't have to worry," she says. "That won't ever happen." She squeezes Glynnis's shoulders. "All done."

Glynnis's hair feels smooth and tight around her face, like it is pulling her mouth back and holding her eyes wide open. "Thank you," she says. But as she leaves the classroom, Glynnis can feel the doubt creeping up the back of her throat. *Ever* is an awfully long time.

Outside, Glynnis looks around for the Megans. They are on the monkey bars, but before she can cross to them, she sees Leora Faust, crouched and shaking on the grass. "Are you sick?" Glynnis asks. "Should I get Miss Glen?"

Leora is on her hands and knees, raking the wet grass with her fingers. When she lifts her head to look at Glynnis, her whole face is red and patchy with crying. "I lost a button," she says between hiccups. "A button off my shirt. I lost it."

"Don't be such a bawlbaby," Glynnis says and glances over her shoulder to make sure the Megans aren't watching. "Get off the ground."

"I'll get in so much trouble," she wails. "You have to help me find it." Leora reaches up and grabs Glynnis's arm with her wet, muddy hand. "Please, Glynnis. Help me."

This is all she needs. If the Megans look over and see Glynnis with Leora, they'll think she *wants* to be here. They'll think she's made a choice. "It's just a button," Glynnis says, but Leora is crying too hard to hear.

Leora slaps the ground, the wet grass sticking to the backs of her hands. "No-no-no-no-*no*," she says. "Oh please, *please* no." Her face is slick with tears and snot and she uses the backs of her wrists to wipe her eyes as she crawls through the grass, smearing wet, grimy streaks across her forehead. Glynnis cannot walk away. She cannot leave her here like this.

"My mom will *kill* me!" Leora shrieks, and Glynnis winces in the direction of the Megans. She leans forward and pretends to look in the grass.

"Maybe it fell off in the classroom," she says. "It's probably on the floor by your desk."

Leora shakes her head, spinning on her knees to feel the grass behind her. "The boys were pulling at my shirt," she says. "When I was over here. It *must* be over *here*!" She is yell-

ing now, choking on her own screechy voice. "Please, Glynnis. Please help me find it."

"Shut up then," Glynnis hisses. "People are looking."

Out of the corner of her eye, Glynnis can see the boys
on the basketball court glancing in their direction. Her ears
prickle with heat and she feels her way down the front of her
blouse until she reaches the last button. It doesn't put up
much of a fight. One good yank, and it pops right off in her
fingers. Glynnis is about to hold it out, about to say, "Here,
you big crybaby, just take this and stop wailing," when Leora
leans forward onto her elbows, her bony spine heaving.

"I won't be able to go to the party now," Leora says, and
Glynnis goes still. "I've never been invited to a slumber party."

Glynnis strokes the button with her thumb and forefinger.
"You haven't?" she asks. "Not ever?"

Leora turns her face sideways on the ground. "I already
got a present and everything." She sniffs. Glynnis squeezes
the button in her palm and Leora turns on her back, letting
one arm fall loosely across her chest. "I got her a book of
different braids she can do with her hair," she says. "It came
with ribbons and sparkly barrettes and things. I thought her
mom could use it when she does her and Megan C.'s hair
before school."

Leora raises one knee and her skirt falls up around her white
thighs. Glynnis looks away, embarrassed. Can't Leora see the
way things are? Did she ever stop to wonder why Megan R.,
who, as far as Glynnis can tell, has never said a single nice
thing to Leora, would suddenly invite her to a birthday party?
No. She just went running out and bought a present.

Glynnis feels the button, smooth and silky between her
fingers. It is nothing, really—a piece of plastic. She looks
down at Leora, at the wet skirt tangled around her muddy legs,

the hint of underpants peeking out beneath the bunched-up hem, and suddenly Glynnis hates her. She hates Leora for being so weak, for making it so easy. Glynnis squeezes the button in her fist. "I don't think we're going to find it," she says.

When the recess bell rings, Leora stands up, her bare legs streaked with dirt and grass. As they file into the classroom, Miss Glen sighs through her teeth and points at Leora. "You're a mess," she says. "Go to the girls' room and clean yourself up."

Glynnis keeps her head down as she pushes her shoes off in the doorway. On her way to her desk, she opens her hand and lets the button fall into the trash can.

Glynnis is waiting for the school bus when her father's car pulls up in the parking lot. "Why aren't you at work?" Glynnis asks.

"Come on," he says to her. "It's starting to rain."

Glynnis climbs into the car and mud flakes off her shoes onto the floor. "I thought we could go get something to eat," her father says. "Just you and me. We can go to a restaurant and order whatever we want. It'll be like a date." Glynnis can feel the grumbling in her stomach and she thinks of a warm, cozy booth where they will share French fries and get cheesecake for dessert. But then she thinks of her mother, alone and naked in the new house, waiting for her.

"I have homework," she says.

"It's Friday," her father tells her. "You have the whole weekend."

"I have a lot," she says. "We start the Civil War next week."

Her father sighs. "Fine," he says.

When they come through the front door, Glynnis's mother walks into the living room, tying her bathrobe around her waist. Her lips are purple with wine. "What are you doing here?" she asks.

Her father stands in the front hallway, looking through the mail. "I took the afternoon off," he says without looking up. "I picked Glynnis up from school."

Her mother nibbles at the rim of her paper cup. "What happened to your hair?" she asks, and Glynnis reaches back to feel her braid.

"Miss Glen did it for me," she says.

"Looks nice," her father says without lifting his head.

"I lost a button," Glynnis tells her mother and holds out the bottom of her blouse. "At school. It fell off or something."

Her mother glances down at the shirt. "Throw it away," she says, and Glynnis's father looks up. Her mother smiles at him. "Daddy'll buy you a new one."

When the phone rings, Glynnis leaves her parents staring at each other in the front hallway to answer. It's Megan R.

"Glynnis?" she says. "Leora's mom just called. Leora can't come to my party."

Glynnis can feel her heartbeat in her throat. "I didn't think her mother would really say no just because of a button," she says, and there is silence on the other end of the phone.

"What?" asks Megan. "She's sick, that's what her mom said."

"Sick?" Glynnis asks. "She seemed fine at school."

"I guess so," says Megan. "But who cares? I told my mom all about you, about how you're new, but you're supercool and she said you can come instead of Leora. Isn't that the best news ever?"

Glynnis says that it is. Maybe Leora really is sick. She *did* spend all that time rolling around on the wet grass. And if she *is* sick, it would only make things worse to lock her outside after she had wet herself.

"I know it's last-minute," Megan tells her. "But my mom says we can come pick you up, if that makes it easier."

When Glynnis walks back to her parents, they are still in the front hallway. Her mother is stroking the collar of her robe with one hand and balancing her paper cup in the other. "That was Megan R.," Glynnis says. "Inviting me to her slumber party tonight." She pulls at her mother's arm. "We have to hurry," she tells her. "We need to find a present."

Her mother looks at her blankly. "You'd spend the night?" she asks. "The *whole* night?"

"It's a slumber party," Glynnis says again, and her mother bites her lip.

"I don't know," she says and holds one hand to her forehead. "I don't think I want you to do that." Glynnis opens her mouth, but before any words come out, her father interrupts.

"Why?" he asks, and Glynnis and her mother look at him. "Why can't she go?"

Her mother shakes her head and turns to walk into the den. Glynnis and her father follow. "I don't know these people," she says. "And I won't have her going off with strangers."

"You can meet them," Glynnis tells her. "And then they won't be strangers."

Her mother chews her purple lips with her teeth. "I want you here," she says in a small voice. "With me."

"Don't do this," her father says, and his voice is low and serious. "Do it to yourself if you have to, but don't do it to Glynnis."

"What are you talking about?" her mother asks and turns to face her father.

"This is home now," he says. "We live *here*."

"Whose fault is *that*?" her mother asks, and her face tightens into something mean and ugly. Glynnis watches her father straighten and broaden across the shoulders, making himself look larger than he is. Her knees begin to wobble. Her hands and feet go cold.

"It's just for one night," she whispers, but no one is listening.

"You," her father says. "You're the one who said we had to move. I would have stayed. But you said no."

Glynnis looks at her mother. This can't be true. It can't be.

Her mother's head snaps up and her eyes narrow. "You and Katie Bell," she says. "How could I have stayed after that?"

"We've talked about this," her father says in a low voice. "It was *over*. I *made* my choice."

Her mother drops her chin to her chest and squeezes her paper cup until it caves in on one side. "You took *everything*," she whispers. "You let them laugh at me."

Her father goes still. "No one was laughing at you," he says, and his voice is softer. "They were your friends. They were never laughing."

Glynnis's mother begins to cry, and her father reaches for her. But as his hand closes around her arm, she yanks away and her paper cup tilts sideways, spilling red wine in an arc across the white carpet. Her mother looks down at the spill, then drops the cup to the floor and runs out of the room.

Glynnis and her father stand, staring down at the stain. "Go," he says to Glynnis. "Go see if she's all right."

Glynnis looks for her mother in the bedroom, but she isn't there. She calls down the hallway and peeks around corners. She is about to go back to her father, about to tell him that her mother must have snuck out the back door, but then she passes the bathroom. The door is open a crack and it is dark inside. As Glynnis edges the door open, a bar of light falls across the tile floor and on the other side of the bathroom, she can make out the shape of her mother in the darkness, sitting in the bathtub.

As Glynnis creeps across the floor, the toe of her shoe catches on the silk of her mother's bathrobe, which is lying like a dark puddle on the floor. Her mother sits with her knees pulled to her chest, naked in the empty bathtub.

"Mum?" Glynnis whispers, but her mother is shaking, her head lowered over her bare knees. She doesn't look up. "Mum, are you okay?"

Her mother doesn't answer, doesn't move, doesn't make a sound. Her skin looks blue in the darkness and her hair spills in messy tangles down the ridge of her spine. Glynnis stands, watching. Those are her mother's hands, her mother's ankles, her mother's narrow shoulder blades. Glynnis has seen her mother's body so many times that it is as familiar as her own. She knows every curve and angle, every knobby joint. But standing in the bathroom, Glynnis stares at her mother and feels nothing. She is a stranger. Glynnis has never seen her before in her life. She backs out of the room and closes the door, leaving her mother there, alone in the darkness.

When Glynnis walks back into the den, her father is on his hands and knees, scrubbing at the stain with a paper towel. The red wine is turning black on the carpet and the paper towel is shredding into scraps as her father rubs harder and harder. *That won't work,* thinks Glynnis, but she doesn't say anything.

"Well?" her father asks without looking up.

"She's fine," Glynnis says. "She just wants some time to herself." Her father nods at the stain, and Glynnis kneels beside him. She watches his hand move across the spill, pressing the pieces of paper towel into the carpet, trying to mop up what has already been absorbed, trying to fix what will be there forever.

Outside there is the low rumble of a car pulling into the driveway, the slam of a car door. Glynnis leans her shoulder against her father's and puts her hand over his. "The party, Daddy. Can I go?"

Boys and Girls
Like You and Me

for N

My best friend is dating an actor. She has dated lots of people, and this is not the first actor, but he's the first actor I've heard of. Unlike her other boyfriends—the lawyer, the performance artist, the Persian poet, the other, less attractive lawyer—I can picture the actor. But I picture him as I've seen him in movies, and he has not been in a movie for fifteen years. Maybe twenty. The actor used to be a child actor, but not a cute one—never the lead. He was odd-looking, skinny with a long neck and a beaky nose. In movies, he always played the weird kid, the unpopular kid, the kid who got beaten up by stronger, better-looking kids.

Gina says that her actor is not an actor anymore, but he is still weird-looking. They met a few days ago when Gina came home from work and found him outside her apartment door, trying to pick her lock with a hairpin. Apparently, he lives in the apartment above Gina's and on the night they met, he was drunk and had gotten his floor confused with hers. When he couldn't make his key work, he tried to pick the lock.

"Why did he have a hairpin?" I ask.

Gina says that the hairpin is not the point of the story. The point of the story is that Gina lives in New York, and in New York, these sorts of things happen all the time. In New York, you can leave your apartment as a single woman and come back to find a burglar who is really an actor who then becomes your boyfriend. New York is a playground, Gina tells me. Disneyland for grown-ups. I should move to New York.

The first time I met Gina, she was high on mushrooms and lying facedown on the living room floor of her college apartment. "It's a *bran muffin!*" she told me, slapping the grubby brown carpet with her open hands. "I'm lying on a giant *bran muffin!*" Now she has a job in the city, not a great job, not a job in her field—but a job. She makes money and pays her bills on time and knows many interesting people who do many interesting things. "I'm worried about you," she tells me on the phone. "I'm worried that you never leave that shitty little apartment, that you never see anyone."

This is the year that everyone is worried about me. I have moved to a town where no one knows me and work online, writing term papers for college students. The pay is crappy, but it's work that I can do in my pajamas while I drink gin and tonics and watch old episodes of *The Real World*.

I tell Gina that she should not worry—I leave the apartment all the time. Daily. Bidaily at the very least. I see plenty of people: the Vietnamese couple across the hall, the single mother and her vampire daughter downstairs, the hillbillies in 2E, all of whom are obese and ugly with brown, rotten teeth, but otherwise perfectly nice. Also, there's David.

Gina snorts. "David."

For a moment, there is silence and I wonder if we've lost our connection. But then Gina sighs and says, "I hate that you're living in that dump."

She has never been to this town, but it is a dump—flat and gray, full of gas stations and parking lots and fast food joints that don't bother to correct their signs after kids change them in the night (*Get Pot Here* advertises the sign outside KFC, and the one in front of Baskin Robbins says *Dixie Riddle has crabs*).

I tell Gina that she should visit. There's a hot springs a couple hours away and a pretty good Mexican restaurant.

Another stretch of silence follows, and, again, I start to think I've lost her.

"Sometimes," she says finally, "I'm worried that you have a brain tumor."

The thing about writing college papers for other people is that it helps to be a little drunk while you're doing it. Most people who pay someone else to write their midterm on the themes of pride and prejudice in the novel *Pride and Prejudice* are not that bright to begin with, so it's best not to overthink.

I found this job through my previous job, which also paid me to work online with college students' essays, only for that job I was not writing the papers but "improving" them. Every correction had to be masked as cheery instruction. Every edit conversational ("The previous sentence is a fragment, Joe. A fragment occurs when a sentence is incomplete. Let's fix it together!").

I am better suited for this job than that job.

When I really get rolling, I can crank out six or seven essays a day—my record is eleven. "Symbolism in *Moby-Dick*" and "Irony in *Catch-22*," "Misogyny in the Comedies of Shakespeare" and "The Color Purple in *The Color Purple*": They practically write themselves.

Once in a while the assignment will ask for a personal essay, and that can be tricky. Professors want papers on life-changing experiences. Most of the time, I don't know anything about the life of the person whose paper I'm writing—not their name or even their gender. And so I write about life-changing events that could happen to anyone, small triumphs and bland tragedies, the death of a childhood pet or the illness of a grandparent, an encounter with a benevolent stranger, a senior trip where we learned a lot about each other and grew so much closer as friends.

I could find a better job—one that pays more money—but I would have to work set hours at a set location, and this is something I cannot do. My boyfriend, David, lives in another town and is married to another woman. When he can get away to come see me, it is always last-minute and for a very short period of time. I keep an open schedule.

At the video store in the strip mall across from my apartment, I rent the only movie they carry with Gina's actor. The girl working the register is the teenage vampire from my apartment building, and when I set the movie on the counter, she looks down without touching it. She is pale and razor-thin, with dark, frightening eye makeup and dyed black hair that falls over her face like a hood. "Have you seen this movie?" she asks, and I say that I have. "This movie's fucked-up."

I ask if she remembers the guy who plays the brother, and she squints, thinking.

"The one who kills himself at the end?"

"My best friend is dating him."

Her eyes widen, the whites stark against the black rims of makeup. "*Shut up,*" she whispers. "That guy is like, *thirteen*."

"No," I say, disappointed that I have not impressed the vampire but merely confused her. "This movie's twenty years old. That guy's a grown-up now. Like me."

She runs one hand through her hair, and when it lifts away from her face, I realize that she's younger than I thought—fourteen, fifteen at most. This surprises me because I have more than once seen her drunk outside the apartment building, kissing her boyfriend and, on one occasion, puking in the bushes.

"I live in the apartment above yours," I tell her, and she says that she knows. She's seen me at the mailboxes. I introduce myself, and she points to her nametag: Iris.

When she pushes the video across the counter at me, her nails are short and jagged, her cuticles raw. I should make sure to return the movie by Friday, she tells me. The late fees here are ridiculous.

The sky in this town is the color of concrete, and the air smells like grease and diesel fumes. My apartment is on the very outskirts, near the airport and the interstate. At night, I lie in bed reading books for work (*A Separate Peace, The Turn of the Screw, Emma*) and listening to the planes coming and going overhead, the semitrucks whistling past.

Night is the time I like best—late night, when the building falls still around me and the traffic quiets on the street. I sometimes pass the whole night on the fire escape, drinking and smoking and looking out over the dark storefronts and empty parking lots.

I drink more than I used to. More than I should. Gin or vodka, mostly. Anything straight from the freezer, anything that chills or numbs. I'm not an alcoholic. I'm only passing time.

When I open my apartment door, I am expecting the UPS man, but instead it's the vampire from downstairs. She is dressed in baggy jeans and a T-shirt, with black rubber bracelets like spiderwebs up the length of both bony arms. "Violet," I say.

"*Iris*," she corrects me, and I repeat this silently in my head: *Iris*.

"Your movie was due back three weeks ago," she says. "You owe a jillion dollars in late fees."

Fuck.

Iris says that she'll return the movie for me. As long as I never try to rent there again, I can probably get away with not paying the fee.

She sits on my sofa and watches while I sift through piles, searching for the rental. I can feel her gaze moving around the room. The coffee table is covered with dirty dishes and empty liquor bottles, the floor littered with piles of unopened mail. I haven't showered in three days.

"Have you been sick?" she asks, and I lie and say I have.

She points to the corner where David's guitar is propped— the only thing in my apartment that belongs to him. "That yours?" she asks, and I tell her it belongs to a friend.

"The guy who was here last week?"

I turn to look at her, and she shrugs. "I've seen him here before," she says. "He helped me catch my cat once."

Iris says that she would like to play the guitar. Right now she takes violin lessons and plays in her school orchestra, but that's only because her grandmother pays for her lessons. If it was up to her, Iris says, she would play the guitar.

She cannot stay and wait while I keep looking for the movie. Her boyfriend is waiting downstairs. His name is Kurt and he races dirt bikes. If she keeps him waiting too long, he makes her buy him dinner.

"He sounds like a prince," I tell her, and her eyes link with mine for a long moment before she slips out the door.

Over the next week, Iris comes back three or four times, but I cannot find the video. She makes halfhearted attempts to help me look, but mostly she picks at her cuticles and talks about her relationship with Kurt, which is fraught with passion and pain. Kurt takes her for granted and makes her pay for everything. All he wants to talk about is racing dirt bikes. Once, when he was drunk, Kurt threw up in her hair.

Still, Kurt is better than her last boyfriend, Mike, who made her have sex with him in his parents' bed.

I stare at her, horrified. "What grade are you in?"

"Ninth."

"And you have sex?" I ask.

Iris rolls her eyes. "Please," she says. "I've been having sex since I was ten."

Later, on the phone, I tell Gina that I feel like I should do something.

"You should," she says. "You should stay out of it."

People sometimes meet for a reason, I tell her, and maybe

there is a reason that I have met Iris. I wonder if I should talk to her mother.

Gina sighs into the phone. "You used to be so interesting. You used to have goals."

"I still have goals," I tell her.

"Yeah," she says. "But now they're fucked-up."

It's three in the morning and I am just finishing an essay on the Lilliputians and what Gulliver should have learned from them when someone knocks on my door. When I open it, Iris is collapsed against my doorframe, sobbing. Her eye makeup runs down her white cheeks in black, muddy rivers, and she reeks of beer and cigarette smoke. I try to help her up and her body leans into mine, sharp and angular as a tangle of wire clothes hangers.

"Kurt dumped me," she hiccups. "Your light was on."

Inside, I make her drink water while she crouches on my sofa in the fetal position, weeping into her knees. Maybe Kurt wasn't perfect, she tells me. But she loved him. Really, she did. She always tried to put him first and do what he wanted. And now he's left her for Dixie Riddle.

"Not Dixie Riddle who has crabs?" I ask, and Iris nods miserably.

She doesn't really have crabs, though, Iris tells me. Someone just wrote that to be mean because Dixie Riddle is a prodigy. Last year she placed first in a national violin competition and was on PBS and *Good Morning America*.

"You're kidding," I say.

Iris and Dixie have been in orchestra together since fifth grade, she says, and Dixie is so good it's sickening. She plays concertos by Beethoven and Tchaikovsky—do I have any

idea how hard it is to play concertos by Beethoven and Tchaikovsky?

I don't, but I nod anyway.

Also, Iris says, Dixie Riddle is nice to everyone and has
shiny blond hair and is a virgin. Iris's mouth wrenches open
as her body spasms into a fresh wave of tears. How can she
possibly compete with Dixie Riddle?

If it makes her feel any better, I say, a lot of prodigies end
up going crazy.

Eventually, Iris runs out of tears and she rolls over onto
her side, resting her head on one arm and staring blankly
across my living room. Sometimes, she says, life just feels too
fucking long.

Iris's mother leaves a note on my door asking me to meet her
for coffee, and I think it is a good sign. Her kid is at my apartment all the time. We should at least know what the other
looks like.

What I know about Iris's mother from Iris is that she works
long hours as a waitress and suffers from sciatica and is very
unhappy. I imagine that I will meet this woman for coffee
and we will have a somewhat awkward but cordial conversation in which we exchange basic information. Maybe she'll be
charmed by me—some people are. Maybe we'll be friends.

Iris's mother is a small woman with mouse brown hair
and a tired, put-upon expression. Her hands have the same
ragged nails and irritated cuticles as her daughter's, and she
tugs at her lower lip with her thumb and index finger while
she waits. The minute I sit down, I can tell that she hates me.

I start to say something obvious about the weather, but
she holds one hand up, stopping me before I can finish.

"Look," she says. "I don't want any trouble with you."

"Okay," I say.

"Iris is fifteen," she tells me. "She's a kid."

"Uh-huh," I say.

"I know you're lonely," she says. "But Iris is young and impressionable. I don't want her around . . ." she leans forward and squints at me as though trying to see me better ". . . whatever it is you do with your time."

My hands are suddenly cold and heavy in my lap. I feel like she just spat at me. "I work for a cheater website."

She gives me a pitying half-smile, then says she has to go.

This time when he leaves, he takes the guitar. He is gone before the sun comes up, and I sit on the fire escape, smoking cigarettes and letting the chill of dawn soak through me. After the pack is empty, I cross the parking lot to the gas station and wait in line behind the high school kids getting their morning Cokes and Pringles on their way to school.

When it's my turn at the register, I don't have enough money for cigarettes. The rims of my eyes feel as though they are full of sand, and when I speak, my voice sounds bruised and husky. "Can you bum me sixty cents?" I croak to the kid behind the cash register.

I hope that he will cover me because he thinks I'm pretty. But when he looks into my face, his lip curls in disgust and he tosses me the cigarettes. "Just take them."

I am almost out of the store when I run into Iris.

"Whoa," she whispers, then reaches into one of the refrigerator doors and pulls out a bottle of Gatorade. "You need electrolytes."

I have no money, but when she puts the bottle in my hand it feels cold and heavy, and all at once, I ache with thirst.

"Put it in your purse," Iris whispers. "Walk out the door."

I glance over my shoulder. The gas station is part of a larger chain and I'm sure there are security cameras. I start to point this out, then remember that Iris is fifteen and impressionable. "I don't steal," I say, and she snorts.

"What?" I ask.

"It's none of my business," she says primly.

"What isn't?" I ask, and she raises her eyebrows.

"David?" I say finally. "You think that what I'm doing with him is the same thing as stealing Gatorade?"

She shrugs.

"Yeah, maybe," I tell her, "maybe it's the same thing. Only for it to be the same thing, this bottle of Gatorade would have to kiss me in a bar. It would follow me home and I would be all, 'No, Gatorade, no, we can't.' And then I would move two time zones away and seven days later Gatorade would say it was going on a business trip and show up at my door."

"And you would drink it."

"I'm thirsty!" I say. "And there's Gatorade, saying, 'Drink me, drink me, drink me.' Does it make me a thief?"

Iris crosses her arms, unimpressed. "It totally does."

I start to tell her that there are extenuating circumstances, that every situation is more complicated on the inside than it appears from the outside, that things happen without people meaning them to happen. But then I realize that there is no point saying any of this out loud because we are talking about a fucking sports drink.

"Whatever," I say and hand it back to her. "I don't steal from stores."

When we get outside, Iris reaches into her backpack and

pulls out the bottle of Gatorade, waving it in front of my face before tossing it to me. "I sometimes do."

When he finally calls, he says that he will make it all up to me—the time I've spent living like a leper in a cave, all the times he's let me down. We are nearing the end of a rocky path, he says. If I can stick it out a little longer, we will be together. Happily ever after and all that. He's done living in fear, he says. He has booked a flight to come see me next week. He is going to tell his wife.

I don't think about his wife very often. What would be the point? I've never met her, don't plan on ever meeting her. But I've seen a picture of her. In the picture—which was not a very good picture—she was hanging a Christmas wreath.

Once, I dreamed that she kissed me in a parking garage. Or maybe I kissed her. I can hardly remember, it was so long ago.

Gina is calling it quits with her actor. Twice in the time since they started dating he has faked attempts at suicide, and he has never told her she's pretty. "This is the first time I've ever dated anyone who doesn't tell me I'm pretty," she says.

So far, the actor isn't handling the rejection very well. Last night, when Gina got home from work, he had broken into her apartment and peed in her bed.

"You need a better lock," I say.

"What I need," she tells me, "is a big beast of a new boyfriend who will beat the shit out of him."

After we hang up, I climb onto the fire escape to smoke. But before I can light my cigarette, I see a policeman crouched by the Dumpster with his gun drawn. For a moment I think that I am misunderstanding something, that I have wandered suddenly into a television show, but then I see another police-man in the bushes beside the building and another behind a parked car. And then I see them everywhere, on the roofs of the buildings across the street and around the edges of the parking lot. When I make eye contact with the one in the bushes, he holds one finger to his lips and waves me back inside.

In the apartment, there is a knock at my door and I think I am going to faint from fear. There is a criminal loose in the building who is going to hold me hostage and humiliate me and eventually kill me, making every bad thing that's ever happened to me so far in my life seem not very bad at all. But then Iris announces that it's only her, and when I open the door she is standing with a ratty orange cat in her arms. "There are people with guns everywhere," she says, and I pull her inside.

Iris's hair is wild with tangles and her lower lip bulges with a cut she has tried to conceal with lipstick.

"What's happening?" I whisper.

The cat squirms and growls in her arms, and she tight-ens her grip. Probably, she says, the police are busting the meth lab.

"What meth lab?" I ask, and she stares at me for a moment like I'm stupid.

"The one in 2E."

"The hillbillies in 2E have a meth lab?"

Iris blinks at me. "They're not hillbillies," she says. "They're meth heads. And yes, they have a meth lab."

This is my first police bust and I don't know the rules. On television, people cower on the ground and stay away from windows, so Iris and I decide to do the same. My bathroom is the only room in my apartment without windows, and we lock ourselves inside and sit at opposite ends of the empty bathtub.

The cat's name is George, and for the first hour we are locked in the bathroom, he paces and yowls at the door. Iris tells me that she and her mother found George in the parking lot of a Pizza Hut during a snowstorm. Her mother is allergic, but she let Iris keep George anyway. He doesn't really like being an inside cat.

I ask Iris how she cut her lip and she says that someone bit it. She was drunk when it happened—it didn't hurt much.

I imagine the men outside rolling in on our building like a storm, that any moment we will hear the thundering of boots on stairs, then screaming and gunfire. I lean my head back and close my eyes, letting the nausea pass through me in waves: I am going to die in the bathtub of a slummy apartment with a teenage nymphomaniac and a feral cat.

"Maybe we should call the police," I suggest, but Iris rolls her eyes.

"And say what? 'I can see you from my window'?"

We wait an hour and a half, then two. We are so hungry that I crawl on my hands and knees to the kitchen and come back with a jar of peanut butter that we pass back and forth in the bathtub and eat with our fingers.

"Maybe," I say, "whatever's going to happen has already happened and we just didn't hear it."

Iris shakes her head no. "The walls in this place are made of cardboard," she tells me. "Everyone hears everything."

She sometimes hears me, she says. She hears me when I fight with David. She sometimes hears me crying.

I start to say that I watch a lot of television and people on television shows are often fighting and crying, particularly on the sorts of shows I watch, which are trashy. But before I can speak, Iris tells me that I shouldn't worry about it. She still cries every night for Kurt, and she and Kurt were together for only five weeks.

Kurt is no longer with the violin prodigy—Dixie Riddle's appeal as a virgin could last only so long—but he will not take Iris back. His new girlfriend has a kid, Iris says. She dropped out of school last year when she got pregnant and now she works at Taco Bell.

Iris pulls her knees to her chest and circles her arms around them, resting her temple on the knob of one kneecap. When she thinks about Kurt, she says, she feels like her insides are being shredded by razors. Sometimes she imagines killing herself in Kurt's bedroom so that he will know how much he hurt her.

After the third hour we cannot last any longer, and when I creep out of the bathroom and peek from the bedroom window, all the police are gone. Traffic flows as normal. People come and go on the sidewalks below. I'd thought that a conflict with so many dramatic elements would end in screams and blood and breaking glass. But really, it ended the way that most things end: silently, invisibly, without us ever knowing why or how.

Fifteen minutes before I am supposed to pick him up from the airport, he calls to tell me that he isn't on the plane. He thought he could do this. But he can't. He's really sorry.

This is how you ended up here: You were poor or unlucky or unwise. You told a lie or broke a rule or wanted something you weren't supposed to have. You ended up here because you didn't care where you ended up, because you were selfish or impulsive or naïve, because you made a bad decision, not once, but again and again and again and again. You ended up here because you could not see what any idiot could see: This is not a place where people come to build a life—this is a place where people fall apart.

"I can't," I say when I open the door, because whatever it is she wants from me, I cannot give it to her. I cannot stand or breathe or speak or function. I cannot listen to her talk about Kurt.

"I need a ride," Iris says, and when I look at her, my stomach flips. Her eyes are red, her lips raw and swollen. Beneath her hair, her throat is striped with bruises.

"What happened?" I ask, and she tells me that I have to drive her to a high school across town. The regional music festival is today. She is supposed to play her violin in front of a judge. She is supposed to do this twenty minutes from now. She can't find her mom.

I cover my ears with my hands. This is not my problem. But then Iris opens her mouth and a gurgle of anguish rises from her throat. "Please," she begs. "Please help me."

The high school is in a part of town I have never been to, with large, shaggy trees and old Victorian houses with pillars and porches and shutters. "Wow," I say, and Iris nods.

"This is a nice town," she tells me. "We just live in the shit part of it."

The regional high school music festival is a pretty big deal and we can't find parking within twelve blocks of the place. So we have to run. Iris's violin case beats against her legs and my lungs ache. When we reach the building we stand pant-ing outside it.

The hallways of the school are filled with students and instruments and parents congratulating their children on jobs well done. I feel a sudden sinking as I realize that everyone is dressed nicely, men in sports jackets and women in heels. All the high school musicians look clean and polished, hair combed, cheeks flushed with health. I am wearing sweat-pants and flip-flops. Iris's black dress is too large for her and it has a stain on the skirt. Her ankles are dirty.

I shouldn't come in with her, Iris tells me as we search for the classroom where she will play. The only people inside are usually the judge and the other musicians playing in that time slot. But when we find Iris's classroom the hallway outside is clogged with people. "This is the room!" someone shouts from down the hall, and a mob of people rushes toward the door.

Iris pushes her way to the wall where the schedule of com-petitors is posted on a sheet of paper. I look over her shoulder and see her time slot, her name, and the name directly after hers: Dixie Riddle.

Iris gapes at the paper. "Fuck me."

Inside the classroom, Iris sits up front with the other three students—two anemic-looking boys and the legendary Dixie Riddle. For a high school girl, she's got it together. Pretty face. Lush hair. She already knows the world belongs to her.

And the crowd packs in to see her. *There she is. That's Dixie. Oh my God. Hi, Dixie. Good luck.*

Iris sits with one leg twisted around the other, her shoul-ders caved, her hair shiny with grease. She lifts one hand to her mouth, sawing at her cuticles with her teeth.

The boys play, first one, then the other, both awkward and

lurching but good enough, and then Iris stands in front. She says her name and her age and her school, and in the crowd I see people exchanging glances as they notice her swollen lips, her neck streaked with bruises.

But as soon as she begins to play, I feel the whole energy of the room roll toward her. Her body, usually so concave, is straight and graceful as she plays, her eyes half-closed, her gaze set somewhere beyond the room. It is evident by her concentration that the piece is difficult. And yet she plays it. She plays it like it's more than notes. She plays it like it's music.

Walking back to the car, the sun is shining through the autumn leaves, streaming down in shafts of gold and yellow.

Iris walks a few paces ahead of me, swinging her violin case gently beside her. "I didn't expect you to be so good," I say, and she smiles.

"I guess I'm pretty good," she tells me. "I've been taking lessons for a long time." Then she turns a pirouette on the sidewalk, and the leaves fall around her, catching in her hair.

That apartment, that town, it wasn't a place where anyone stayed. One way or another we would both be gone soon. Neither of us would ever go back.

And so I wish now that I could have that day to live again, that golden walk to the car. I should have told you how the light fell on you in that classroom, the way the atmosphere softened and brightened around you as you played. And— how had I never seen it before?—you were so beautiful and elegant and beloved. In the moment you played the last note, your bow still quivering over the string, that hot, crowded room drew a collective breath and I cannot recall a fuller, more radiant moment in my life.

And this, this is the part I want you to know: That moment lives in my head, a thing with breath and blood. A present tense. An always—that sudden blossoming of grace and beauty and competence, all of it so unexpected, all of it so undeserved, and the feeling or knowledge or faith that somehow, someday, everything was going to be all right.

Acknowledgments

Much thanks to my fellow workshoppers in the MFA program at the University of Montana, who helped me through the early drafts of many of these stories. Similarly, I would like to thank the workshops at the Sewanee and Bread Loaf writers' conferences, both of which gave me invaluable advice and inspiration at times when I was in desperate need of them. Finally, I could not have written this book without the generosity of the Rona Jaffe Foundation or the time I spent at the Millay and MacDowell colonies, or without the support and good humor of my friends and family—thanks to all.

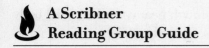

Boys and Girls Like You and Me

Questions for Discussion

1. Discuss how love appears in its many forms (physical, romantic, unrequited, etc.) throughout these stories. To better center your discussion, try selecting two or three stories on which to focus your group's attention. Do these stories cast love in a negative light? A positive one?

2. "Femme" is the only story in this collection without a clear central character. Rather, it is narrated by an elusive "we," or "us." How does not having a specific central character affect the tone of the story?

3. Similarly, "Captain's Club" is the only story in this collection with a male as the central character. Does the story still speak to the female experience? If so, how?

4. In "Allegiance," Glynnis's mother has tried to escape her husband's past wrongdoings by moving her family to America. Is her escape successful? Do you think she can eventually learn to be happy in her new home?

5. Consider Kyle's young protagonists, those dealing with the difficulties of elementary- or high-school life. Does their youth make their troubles less serious or authentic? Why or why not?

6. The authority figures (teachers, parents, etc.) in these stories have a strong impact on the children in their lives. Which of these authority figures have the most positive impact, and which the most negative? Are any of these authority figures aware of the impact they can have? Which?

7. "But when, at last, Tommy began to cry, it was not because of fear or loneliness or disappointment, but because there

was so much beauty, too much beauty for his small body to hold." This excerpt is from the poignant final paragraph of "Captain's Club." How is Tommy changed by the red light of the moon? Why did C.J. refuse to see it?

8. Kyle explores the relationship between sisters in "Economics" and "Take Care." How is the dynamic between the sisters in these two stories similar? How is it different? Now add Dilly and her older sister, from "Brides," to the mix. How does their relationship compare to the first two?

9. A sister and brother's tenuous relationship hits a new low in "Company of Strangers." How does the introduction of a brother figure change the sibling relationship? Who is to blame for what happens in this story: the sister, the brother, or neither?

10. Which characters in these stories, if any, are truly happy?

11. Have each member of the group pick a character with whom they feel the most connected. Then, discuss: What is it about this particular character that feels relatable?

Enhance Your Reading Group

1. In "A Lot Like Fun," Leigh asks her class of second-graders, "What's the most important thing?" Have the members of your group make a list of most-important things, and discuss why these things are so important. Did the second-graders' answers of "chocolate, mothers, and Nintendo" make the list? What might you have said when you were in second grade?

2. As you discuss each story in this collection, ask the members of your reading group to think about the following question: What song best represents the mood of this story? After making a list of the suggested songs, create a playlist or mix CD for each member of the group to have.